THE COMANCHE'S REVENGE

For over twelve years, Kit Bayfield believed his son was dead. Back then, Kit's two other sons had been unable to find Mitch. But now, an Indian claiming to be his son, and going by the Comanche name of Broke, confronts him. Kit reckons folks will find Broke's return difficult. Everyone should have helped search for the boy and now his son's face is full of hatred — the whole town, including his brothers, is on his payback list . . .

D. M. HARRISON

THE COMANCHE'S REVENGE

Complete and Unabridged

LINFORD
Leicester

First published in Great Britain in 2012 by
Robert Hale Limited
London

First Linford Edition
published 2013
by arrangement with
Robert Hale Limited
London

A catalogue record for this book is available
from the British Library.

ISBN 978–1–4448–1740–9

Published by
F. A. Thorpe (Publishing)
Anstey, Leicestershire

Set by Words & Graphics Ltd.
Anstey, Leicestershire
Printed and bound in Great Britain by
T. J. International Ltd., Padstow, Cornwall

This book is printed on acid-free paper

1

He sat astride his Appaloosa horse, his Henry rifle aimed at the old man's heart. The gun held sixteen bullets, more than enough to blast the feller to pieces, if he decided to use it.

'My handle's Kit Bayfield, stranger. I own this here ranch. What do you want?'

He acted outwardly calm, yet the smell of fear hovered round him. The eyes darted here and there, on the look-out for an escape route. Beads of perspiration formed under his hatband and ran down his brow. He rubbed the palms of his hands dry on the sides of his britches.

'I've come to collect on a debt owed,' the stranger said.

He noted a smile light up Kit Bayfield's face as a wave of relief washed over.

'I can give you anything you want. Gold, greenbacks,' he said.

It was almost a shame to disappoint him and see the fear come back.

'You've not got enough money to pay this debt.'

Kit Bayfield took in the stranger's appearance. 'I got plenty of beads, firewater . . . ' he continued.

For his answer, he heard the sound of a trigger guard being released on the stranger's rifle.

'I'm not an Indian,' he said.

Whatever the stranger's words, it was plain by the look on Kit Bayfield's face that he was convinced the man was an Indian. He was dressed in buckskin pants with a jacket open to reveal a bare muscular chest, had moccasins on his feet and his hair, under his bowler hat, was greased with bear oil and hung down over his shoulders in two plaits.

To Kit Bayfield, that spelt Comanche.

His mind went back to that God-awful attack on their ranch many years ago. After that, the army had negotiated a treaty with the Indians and gradually moved them out towards the reservations. Not all went willingly — the Comanche especially hated the loss of their lands — and Kit figured they'd caused a lot of trouble for everyone. It was with these thoughts in his mind that he tried to work out what the stranger wanted. However, he couldn't have imagined he'd hear the words the stranger uttered.

'I'm your son.'

A myriad of emotions distorted Kit Bayfield's features as he stared up at the stranger. His son, Mitch, had died over twelve years ago. This was a Comanche Indian. Yet he noticed the chestnut colour of his hair, same as Dolcie, Mitch's ma, and the cold ice-blue eyes, same as his, staring out of a face browned by years living out on the plains. They didn't belong to an Indian.

'Mitch?'

'Yes, but I'm known by my Comanche name, Broke,' he answered.

Kit Bayfield's ruddy face blanched

white. He knew he could be facing death as he looked at the barrel of the rifle and begged him to hear him out.

'Your brothers, Russell and Tyler, they went looking for you.'

Broke's eyes didn't leave Kit Bayfield's face. He looked hard to find the truth behind the words and see into the old man's soul. He didn't remember this man. The man with red rheumy eyes, and cheeks and nose painted red by too much sun and liquor. His pa had been a man shaped by hard work, strong in body and mind.

'They said they couldn't find you. I searched, but eventually we just got on with our lives. There was nothing else to do. For all these years I believed my son's — I mean your grave — was in the desert.' His gaze went towards the edges of his ranch. It was as if he could see the very spot from where he stood. 'I used to ride out there day after day. I nigh on lifted every blade of grass to find you.'

Broke saw the old man told the truth,

as he knew it. Many years of living as the adopted son of a great warrior, had given him insight into a man's character. He recalled Fighting Bear's words, a man of great wisdom, who'd said 'don't pass judgment on a man until you've walked a mile in his moccasins'. He'd walked for twelve years in this man's shoes and felt he could make the right judgment. Kit Bayfield wasn't a man who lived with the fear his past would catch up with him, he was someone who'd lived with sorrow. He lowered his Henry rifle and placed it into his saddle holster. His hand moved to pull the reins of his horse but Kit Bayfield called out to him.

'Wait. Please come into my home, your home, and sup with me,' he said.

'Thank you, but I have to find my brothers.'

'You won't find them round here,' Kit Bayfield said. Broke's demeanour gave the impression that it didn't matter, that he'd wait. His pa tried to defend his other two sons. 'They were only young.'

Broke was unimpressed. 'They were my age when they came searching,' he said. 'And although they were ready to turn about before exhausting every place I might be, I won't do the same. Please give them a message from me.' Kit Bayfield waited, expecting the worst. He received it. 'I'll not stop searching. Unlike my brothers, who gave up so easily, I'll circle the earth to find them.'

Broke's hand briefly touched his smooth, low-crowned bowler hat, then turned his horse with a flick of the reins and a gentle press of his knees.

Riding out, the sign fixed over the main gate, 'The 3 Bay Ranch', didn't go unnoticed by Broke. Although his expression stayed the same, a tell-tale sign of his anger — a thin blue vein at the side of his face — pulsed faster than before. He wondered how long it had taken his two half-brothers to repaint the sign. He'd bet it was as soon as they'd returned home without him that 4 Bay had been changed back to 3.

Kit Bayfield watched him leave the ranch. They both knew he'd lied when he said he had no idea of Tyler or Russell's whereabouts. It was difficult having lost one son; to give up two more was unthinkable. He couldn't imagine that Mitch would ever be his 'son' again. He was as lost to him now as he'd been before.

Tyler and Russell said they were going out with the cowhands. In truth, Kit knew well enough that Russell was around somewhere nursing a bottle of whiskey and Tyler was probably off frequenting his favourite gambling saloon. They'd both got out of control after Mitch went missing. At first they all acted out a semblance of normality — turned things around and rebuilt the ranch, got a big spread of land and cattle together — but there was always a ghost hanging about the place, a ghost who shouted at them all, 'You left me to die'.

Kit Bayfield looked where Broke was headed.

The townsfolk would find his return a difficult one. Everyone who lived there knew they should've played a part in searching for the boy.

And, from the rigid set of the shoulders on the receding figure, as far as his long lost son was concerned, it wasn't only his brothers he had a quarrel with; he reckoned the whole town was on his payback list.

2

The town, aptly named 'Hell' — right in the middle of the prairies and sandwiched somewhere between the Pecos River and the Rocky Mountains — got its nickname a long time ago.

It wasn't a good name but sometimes things stick.

The whole area around Pecos County was said to be hell.

The prairies were burning hot in summer and freezing cold in winter. The Pecos river-banks were littered with the bodies of cattle that'd heard the water but couldn't see it. Maddened by thirst, they were uncontrollable and many plunged headlong down its steep sides and drowned in the river, or stuck in quicksand banks without even tasting the water.

There was a place that led from 3 Bay Ranch to town, called Dead Man's

Gulch, a deep V-shaped valley with plenty of hidden dangers. In parts it was narrow and winding, full of places for the unwary to slip down to the bottom of the ravine. Its river, twisting along the bottom of the narrow valley, seemed to disappear into a vapour under the hot prairie sun.

The fact was that the river cut so deep in the terrain, it really only vanished beneath the ground. Strangers to the place thought there was no water at all — hence its name, Dead Man's Gulch.

It was through this place, from 3 Bay Ranch, that Broke headed towards Hell.

As his horse trotted through, Broke kept his eyes open. He noted every tree, shrub and plant. The sounds he heard were grasshoppers rubbing their back legs like they were trying to play a violin, the cry of the red-tailed hawk and the creak of his leather gun holster. He enjoyed the musical interlude but knew outward appearances were deceptive and there were plenty of places for where he could be dry-gulched.

Then his horse's body trembled and its ears flattened against its head. There was a perfect accord between man and beast. The magnificent animal, with its deep brown coat that mellowed to a creamy white as it reached its abdomen and hindquarters, was caught and trained by Broke as a youngster. It was an extension of him. During his sojourn with the Comanche he'd acquired excellent horse skills. The two now reacted together. Broke swung down low so his horse protected his body. He wasn't about to provide an easy target for anyone. The danger, he was certain, would come from above on the left. Out of the corner of his eye, behind a Ponderosa Pine, he saw the sunlight briefly flash on the barrel of a gun.

Broke cursed his failure to check out the ranch. The sight of the old place, albeit rebuilt, and meeting his pa again, had made him incautious. He hadn't taken time to search the ranch's numerous rooms and outbuildings, any one of which could've held danger. Like a fool he'd taken his pa's word about Tyler and Russell. He made a mental note not to trust the old man again. He understood that his pa didn't want to have son against son, but it was inevitable.

Bullets buzzed past his hat like angry bees denied their honeycomb. His horse needed no incentive to go faster. It galloped at high speed across the prairie, with Broke hanging on, and by the time he'd swung back on to the saddle, he was well out of reach of the gunman.

Broke wasted no time looking for the assailant and continued towards his destination. He had a notion that who-ever took a shot at him would be itching to meet up with him again.

At certain times of the year, as the bright prairie sun moved along its path in the sky towards the west, its rays seemed to paint the town. It was purely an optical illusion that the place turned red, but nevertheless it gave folks the shivers-hence its nickname.

It was evening of spring 1873, when Broke rode into Hell. The sun's tendrils had reached down before disappearing below the horizon, and coloured the town red.

He was aware that all eyes were on him, but it didn't faze him. Any stranger who entered town would be scrutinized. Broke knew many wouldn't recall him right off. Last time he'd been here he'd been no more than a ten-year-old nipper. When he reached the marshal's office, he swung off his horse and hitched it to the rail. A square-set man wearing a tin star, came out. The marshal couldn't or wouldn't quite look him in the eye. It might have been because he wasn't as tall as Broke, but it might have been who he'd seen, that disturbed him.

It was the same marshal that had been running the town since as long as Broke could remember. Broke nodded at Marshal Jones. The man didn't return the greeting.

'I hope you ain't planning to stay too long,' the marshal said. It wasn't a question. 'This town doesn't hold too much with Injuns.'

'Seems you need to hear a couple of things, Marshal, to help you out,' Broke said. 'I'm staying as long as I need, to do what I have to do, and further than that I can't tell you. And I'm not an Injun.'

The man was plainly taken aback. Broke ignored the raised eyebrows and lips that pulled into a snarl and confronted the marshal with the truth. 'I used to be known as Mitch Bayfield.'

'That boy who was killed by the Injuns?'

'Yes I supposed Mitch Bayfield was killed, in a way, 'cause my name is Broke. I've come to find my two half-brothers, Tyler and Russell.'

'I don't want any trouble in this town. Whoever you are, you get out of here. And if you're still here by midnight, I'll come gunning for you.'

When the moon replaced the sun

14

over Hell, it sucked every vestige of colour from the wooden buildings to give it an eerie, unworldly quality. That might have accounted for the way the marshal looked now. His hair, highlighted to a strange kind of grey, gave him the appearance of an apparition. Yet it was the marshal who thought he stared at a ghost. Someone the town had put to rest a long time ago had turned up larger than life.

Marshal Jones twisted round on his heel, went back into his law office and slammed the door. If anyone had looked through the window they'd have seen him head for his desk, pull out a bottle of whiskey, and down a couple of large slugs of the fiery liquid.

Broke remounted his horse and made his way along Main Street.

People were wary of staring directly at the stranger who'd arrived in town. He looked like a Comanche with his hair in plaits, but they noticed that the chestnut sheen and the ice-blue eyes, that took everything in a sweeping gaze, belied that fact. It disturbed them, the way he sat on his horse — on a small neat saddle made out of leather and hide, decorated with horn and secured only with a thin strip of hide. It had a holster attached for his rifle. The saddle had no stirrups and the man tucked his moccasin-clad feet against the belly of his horse.

He rode silently, with only the horse clump-clumping as its hoofs hit the soft dirt road. They didn't like his presence at all. It felt as if the man had come looking for someone, and everyone his glance fell on shuddered.

3

A girl walked towards him from one of the saloons. She wore a red satin dress decorated with cream lace. Cut low on the front, it displayed her ample cleavage. The hem was short enough to reveal her knees and on her feet she had short black leather boots.

As she got nearer he saw she wasn't a young girl; she'd seen a lot more years than he'd figured at first glance. The cleavage was crepy and her breasts sagged. Her slim body had thickened around the waist. However, she had more confidence than anyone else and was willing to ask questions.

'What are you doing here?' she asked. 'I heard someone say your name is Mitch Bayfield? Is it true?'

News travelled fast in a small town. He remembered the voice but every-thing else was different. Instead of a neat, shy woman who used to say 'good day' to his ma, Broke discovered a hard-faced female who looked as if she'd fallen on bad times.

'But you don't call yourself that anymore. You got some silly name instead.'

He touched his hat politely to her and wondered how a woman could've changed so much that she'd approach him to rib him about his name.

'You'd best go back into the saloon,' he said.

Thick powder clogged the lines on her face and the red paint bled from her lips, making it look like an open wound rather than a mouth. Her confidence started to evaporate, as he stared at her in a bold manner, but she didn't move away.

'Need to stable my horse,' he said.

'Carry on right to the end of the street.' Broke went to move away from her but he stopped and held his hand out towards her. She didn't hesitate. Her veined hand, marred further by painted nails, reached out and allowed his muscular arm to haul her up beside him. Her arms were fast around his waist and her face nestled against his back. 'I'll show you if you like. I'll show you anything you want to see.'

Her reputation got lost many years ago and she wasn't about to allow any scandalized looks to prevent her from doing exactly what she pleased.

She'd travelled west with the wagon train but lost her husband and two young children on the trail and she'd ended up here, in Hell. She'd tried to earn her living in a decent way but in the end she'd kept body and soul together in the only way known to a lone woman. Some, in the same circumstances, might have bagged a new husband and started all over again, but perhaps — as she told anyone who'd listen when she'd had enough liquor — she had a tiny bit of badness inside her that made sure her ring finger stayed bare.

'You've lived here a long time,' Broke said.

It wasn't a question but that's how she took it. She blinked her eyes, coquettishly. 'Well a feller oughtn't to ask that, but if I recall rightly, I'd say you were a nipper when I arrived in this town. And you've grown into a fine young man.'

Broke hadn't intended to delay his quest, but her invitation was impossible to ignore, and she, like most folk here, owed him. In the darkness of the stables he held her tightly and she expected a kiss but instead he roughly wiped the paint from her face with a neckerchief he pulled from the pocket of his jacket.

'What you do that for?' she asked.

She looked as if she didn't know whether to scream or cry. She did neither, momentarily too shocked to move.

'Leave Hell,' he said. His ma would've been the same age as the woman. 'Get yourself some self-respect and start over again.'

She looked for a moment to Broke like she'd scream. Instead her face pulled into a sneer.

'Mitch, or Broke, or whatever you

20

call yourself now, don't you go and criticize me. You're a boy trying to act the man. You don't know anything about me.' She turned away but not before she handed him some more advice. 'You look as if you need a haircut' — her nose twitched as she added — 'and a bath.'

As she left the stables he wished he could remember her name. Then he shrugged his shoulders. It wasn't time for regrets. Broke's hand went to his long hair. She was right. He ought to get a haircut and clean himself up.

He told the stableman to rub his horse down, give it a drink and some fresh hay and he'd collect it later. He planned to leave Hell as soon as he'd collected on his debts.

The same barbershop as he remembered was still on Main Street. It was as much a fixture as a general store or a saloon. Here a man could sit on a cushioned chair, pick up a newspaper and have a two-bit haircut or a ten-cent shave.

'We're closed. Ain't got time to do any more cutting.' The barber didn't look up from finishing his chore of polishing a customer's personalized shaving mug. Broke recognized the gruff voice and wondered if the man would remember him.

'Maybe you can make an exception for me, Cutler.' The man, broad shoulders and arms like a smithy, stopped midway to hanging the mug on the rack where a whole line of mugs, each emblazoned with a customer's name, hung, and stared at Broke. The expression on his shrewd face said he knew him but couldn't place him anywhere other than in a reservation. And it wasn't everyday he had such a strange sounding customer.

'You look like an Injun but you don't sound like no Injun,' he said.

'And, Cutler, you don't sound like you've got a voice like a nightingale, but when you start singing everyone listens.'

Cutler's ebony skin paled to the

colour of vanilla and his whole body shook.

'W-w-who are you?'

'Haven't been around here for a long, long time. When I came in with Pa I used to pray for the day I could have a proper haircut. Instead, Ma would hack my hair off, using a pudding basin as a guide. Today I'll have that haircut I promised myself.'

'Mitch Bayfield? You're dead and buried,' Cutler said.

'So I've been told. I think the town was happy to believe my half-brothers. Made things a whole lot easier for them.' He sat down on the barber's chair. 'And by the way, the name's Broke.'

He waited for Cutler to give him a haircut. Broke watched the sweat bead across the barber's forehead. Then Cutler took a deep breath before nervously taking a plait of Broke's hair. He nearly closed his eyes tight shut before he sheared it straight off.

'You all right with that?'

Broke was tempted to say 'no', but he merely lifted the other plait towards Cutler. He looked at the man and wondered if he'd ever had any thoughts about what had happened that day. Cutler answered the question as if he'd spoken out loud.

'You know,' he said, 'I always wondered why your half-brothers just stopped looking for you.'

'No one else in town bothered to look for me either,' Broke said.

Cutler hesitated before answering. 'Was it their job to do that?' He fell silent. It wasn't as if there was anything to say that could alter the past. He carried on cutting as if his life depended on it.

'Folks ought to have rallied round and helped out,' Broke said.

'Well, you'll be all right now, your pa and brothers have one of the biggest spreads round here. They'll look after you.'

Broke said nothing. He didn't need to as Cutler carried on talking and snipping hair.

'Sure upsets them folks from Lazy Z Ranch on the next spread. They can't compete with your pa no matter how hard they try. Outfit started up five years ago and, since he bought some land your brothers wanted, he hasn't had a handful of luck.' Cutler's voice went down an octave. 'They've lost more cattle than you can blame on Injuns,' he said. 'We've had some Injun trouble hereabouts recently. Don't know if it's those Comanche, or the Kiowa from further away on the plains, who's responsible. I suppose when they've got a tomahawk against your scalp you don't ask what tribe these bucks are from!'

Again Broke made no comment. He didn't know anything about Indian attacks. Skirmishes between Indians and white settlers always happened. He knew that well enough.

He put his hand to his head.

'It feels as if I'm bald as a coot. Leave some to settle on my collar,' he said.

'It'll grow again and be long enough

to keep out the winter chills,' Cutler said. He never ignored his customer's wishes but felt someone who'd not had a hair-cut for years and kept it smothered with bear grease, ought to have a bit of scalp exposed to the elements.

'If you want I could shave you, Mitch? I mean Broke. What the hell is that for a name anyway?'

The barber laughed at his fuzz and said he didn't know whether he had enough to shave, but then Broke had heard him say that to men over fifty, not just to young'uns, when he'd visited the place with his pa.

Broke looked in the mirror when Cutler had finished cutting and shaving him. He hardly recognized the person staring back at him.

His life as a Comanche Indian was over.

4

Broke left without paying for the haircut and shave.

'You owe me,' he said.

Cutler shrugged his shoulders. He didn't argue.

'On the house.'

The barber had brushed the back of his neck but later when Broke felt little bits of hair sticking into his skin he wished he'd taken up the offer of a twenty-five cent soak in the tub out back, soap and towel included. He'd appreciated the shave and when he ran his hand along his chin it felt good. The Comanche men used to tease him about his beard. They pulled their facial hair out by its roots, disliked anything other than a smooth skin, but he chose to scrape his chin with a knife.

Broke walked along the street and went into the Last Chance Saloon. His feet scuffed the sawdust thrown over the floor to soak up anything that missed the spittoons. He stood at the bar and ordered a drink.

'Make it a beer. Cold and right to the top of the mug.'

He avoided the house rotgut. It was one hundred per cent proof liquor, although sometimes adulterated by unscrupulous barkeeps with turpentine, gunpowder or pepper, to turn it into a potent brew.

'Might manage cool,' the barkeep said. The beer overflowed and ran down the sides of the mug as he poured and talked. 'Spring's a good season but soon alters. In fact the weather's starting to heat up now, can't keep much cool in Hell.'

The barkeep smiled telling his joke about it being too damned hot in Hell.

'How long you worked here?' Broke asked.

He'd never been in the Last Chance Saloon before and wanted to know its history. He felt he ought to find out who'd been around all those years ago.

'Moved here about three years ago.' The barkeep dusted the polished oak top with his apron like a prissy house-proud woman. It didn't need cleaning; no dust or dirt stained the cloth. 'When the owner died last year I decided to buy the place. He died from lead poisoning after being pumped full of bullets.' Again he smiled at his own joke. It plumped up a thin face. 'Never thought I'd own a bar in Hell.'

The barkeep chuckled and his waxed moustache twitched. Broke guessed he had loads of jokes to tell but he put money for the drink on the counter and moved further away. The barkeep owed him nothing from the past but, even taking that into consideration, he reckoned he sure didn't have to listen to his jokes.

The end of the bar was a good vantage point as any to stand, watch, and listen. He placed his trusty Henry on the counter; Marshal Jones hadn't said he couldn't carry a gun, only told him to get out of town by midnight. If trouble called, he wanted to be ready.

Broke didn't know the whereabouts of his two half-brothers, though he wondered if it was one of them who'd taken the pot shot at him in Dead Man's Gulch. Pa wasn't letting on about his brothers but, as he'd waited years to meet up with them, he reckoned he could wait a bit longer. In the time he'd lived with the Comanche, he'd learned that a man could find out a lot by listening to others.

It was the unwritten code of the West — you didn't ask too many questions. It was a place a man could disappear from his past and start all over again, as many times as he wanted to. However, Broke wasn't going to let these two men escape from their past. He aimed to bring retribution right to their door.

The tinkling keys of the piano sounded out a dance tune and, regardless of the time of day, there'd be girls lined up for men to pay for their company. Fifty cents would buy you a couple of turns round the dance floor. As a fairly rare commodity in the West, a girl could earn a lot of money merely dancing the days and nights away. He couldn't see the woman he met in the street and hoped she'd taken his advice — packed up and left town.

Suddenly Broke became aware that he was being watched. He looked across the saloon and saw a man at the swing doors. His frame was narrow at the shoulder and broad at the hips, and he wore a pair of guns strapped across his butt.

Broke believed that you could only really use one gun at a time so an extra gun, most times, was merely for show. He supposed the man knew how to use them because he wore the guns like an extension of his arms. They were Peacemakers, each with a cut-away trigger guard to give the man a split second advantage.

Apart from the Henry rifle, Broke didn't carry a firearm to ensure his personal safety. He'd placed the weapon on the bar next to his hat and his beer.

The man finally entered the Last Chance Saloon. His spurs, strapped to a pair of short black boots, jangled as he walked. He cut a comical figure with his shrunken pants that showed wrinkled pink long-drawers underneath. No one laughed at him.

He appeared to be searching for someone. His gaze alighted on Broke. He directed a question to the barkeep. His manner was insolent, challenging, but Broke kept his own counsel. He had no desire to make conversation or bring attention to himself.

'Don't you know it's against the law to sell liquor to Injuns?' the man asked. He scratched his head and squashed the lice he caught between his thumb and finger. The barkeep looked at the man everyone in town knew as Lester Young and then at Broke.

'He ain't no Injun, Mr Young,' the barkeep said.

The other man leaned forwards across the bar and contradicted him.

'I saw him when he spoke to the marshal. He sure looked like a Injun then.' Everyone in the saloon turned to look at Broke. 'But then he had his hair in long plaits. Sure he's cleaned up some but you can't wash the stink of Comanche away,' Lester Young said. 'We've had enough of Injuns. They raided a homestead two weeks ago. One of them might have been you.'

It was obvious that Lester Young wanted a fight. The barkeep squirmed. He didn't want any trouble in his saloon. He'd bought a fine gilt-edged mirror last month, tastefully decorated with a naked lady, which came all the way from New York. He feared it would be the first thing to get smashed if bullets started flying.

The barkeep pushed the money Broke had given him for the beer across the bar towards him. His hand shook.

'Have that drink on the house,' he said. 'Then leave. Please.'

Broke's gaze never left the man with the guns, as he merely shoved the fifty cents back across toward the barkeep.

'I bought the beer and I'm staying to drink it.'

The barkeep didn't argue. He called a bar-boy to help him take the mirror down, and turn its mercury-coated glass away from the bar, before they slowly edged away.

The gunman's lips squashed into something that could be said to resemble a smile. Truth was, his face would frighten the buzzards off a gut wagon.

'What I love is an Injun needing to be taught a lesson.'

He moved purposely along the bar towards Broke.

In the saloon, the tinkling piano keys sounded a discordant note and the tap, tap, tapping of the girl's heels cracked like shots across the floor. Soon the noises dimmed and the atmosphere thickened with tension as the two men sized each other up. Broke caught the smell of fried salt pork and cornbread.

The man with the Peacemakers with the cut-away trigger guard seemed too hasty in his summary of the 'Injun'. He figured he'd have plenty of time to draw and shoot him. He'd move faster than a man who had to pick up his weapon from the bar in front of him. Lester Young hadn't worked out that someone else, like he did, could carry two weapons. He looked as if he thought the Injun was easy to kill and his hands moved towards his guns.

Suddenly something happened that was too fast for him to comprehend. His neck ballooned in size as blood from his heart tried to find somewhere else to go. His eyes bulged with incomprehension as he looked down and saw a knife sticking into his chest.

It was the last thing he saw.

5

People said that Lester Young, the gunslinger, had more notches on his belt than the years he'd lived. He fired faster than all the men he'd met. A fact, perhaps, that made him careless. It definitely made it certain he'd meet his end with his boots on.

He was intent on killing the Injun. He didn't succeed.

'You killed him!'

Everyone in the saloon was taken aback at the suddenness of the argument, and its end. On the floor, without firing a shot, Lester Young lay dead.

'You killed him!' the barkeep said again.

Broke ignored the comment. He merely finished his beer and pushed the empty vessel towards the barkeep.

'I'll be back for another one later,' he said.

He walked over to Lester Young's body, bent down and pulled his knife from the middle of the man's chest. Young had a look of surprise on his face, like he'd met his Maker but had been rushed along to the appointment before he was ready. Broke's knife had stopped his heart so quickly, Young had had no time to utter even a gasp. Broke stood up straight and turned to see a shotgun being waved at him.

'Not so quick, Mister whatever your name is.' The marshal's angry face glared at Broke. 'I told you to get out of town. Now you've murdered a man.'

Broke didn't move. He didn't speak. He didn't want to give Marshal Jones a reason to shoot him. It was almost as if he'd been outside, waiting and watching, hoping Broke would get mixed up in some kind of trouble. The blood dripped from the knife and pooled on to the floor.

'I'm gonna lock you up until the judge comes and then we'll hang you.'

'This town has already left me for

dead once. You want to do it again? Make sure you succeed this time?'

The colour drained from Marshal Jones's face.

'I don't want that sort of talk,' he said.

Before Broke could respond, a gambler who looked irritated at the interruption to his game of cards, shouted out. He pointed to the man on the floor.

'Why wait for the judge, Marshal? The man on the floor never had time to use his gun.'

'That true?'

The marshal looked about him for more witnesses. From experience he knew if he could find a few more, that would make his job a whole lot easier. And he'd be rid of the stranger who'd come into town. He'd told his deputy he had a bad feeling about the man. He said how the man was a boy returned from the dead. However, things were not going to go his way.

'I saw everything, Marshal Jones.'

The marshal looked towards the owner of the voice.

'What you got to say, Gil Tander?'

'This man would've been full of bullet holes if he hadn't had a knife. His rifle was on the bar the whole time. Lester Young could see that and he wasn't going to give this man time to use it. He got his guns out, ready to fire, and he took his chance, like anyone else who draws. Sometimes it's your last time.'

Broke had noticed the man at the bar as he drank his beer. The cowboy, still wearing leather chaps over a pair of denim pants, said he'd been taking a break from ranch chores for a couple of hours. The marshal lowered his shotgun as Tander said his piece. Tander worked as foreman on the Lazy Z Ranch. He was respected in the town and the marshal knew his boss, Crosland Page, would back him one hundred and ten per cent.

'Well, seems like you've got a witness that said Lester Young drew his gun first,' Marshal Jones said, 'but I still want you out of this town. I think you're a troublemaker.'

The marshal turned and left Broke with Tander.

'I owe you a thank you,' Broke said. He shook the man's hand and then he moved away. He stepped over the dead gunman and walked towards the door. 'Perhaps someone will move the body before the maggots get gnawing.'

'Hey, what are you planning to do now? I know it's bad form to ask a man about his plans, but I figure it won't hurt to offer a job to an Injun, or whatever you are. The ranch needs good men. It's the Lazy Z Ranch.'

Broke stopped by the door.

'Name's Gil Tander,' he said.

'I go by the name of Broke.'

Tander didn't make any comment. As far as he was concerned, people could go by any name they chose.

'You got any horses to tame?'

'Got men rounding them up now. Probably have a corral of wild mustangs when I get back. Our last bronco buster got too many broken bones and decided to quit,' he laughed. 'Boss pays decent wages though.'

'I'm not an Indian, although I lived with the Comanche for a long time,' Broke said. 'My folks own the 3 Bay Ranch, but I left home many years ago.'

Broke measured the man's mettle. Tander had blinked when he'd said he belonged at the 3 Bay Ranch and said the Lazy Z Ranch backed right up to it, but nothing else. He took in the tall, broad frame, similar to his own, but a few years older. He liked the honest look of his weather-beaten face with sharp button brown eyes and decided he could do worse than call him a friend. Broke needed a place to bed down and get a meal. He only wanted the basic things to sustain him. He was not planning to spend much because as far as he figured, the town owed him.

The money he'd spent on beer hadn't bought him any more information than he knew already. Like the fact that some people you can trust and some you can't. If he took the job he'd still have plenty of time to hunt down those who owed him big time.

Broke nodded. Like it was a good idea. A spread that joined the 3 Bay Ranch was as good as any to stay.

'I'm heading to the Lazy Z Ranch in an hour, and as the marshal don't like you none, you could do worse than come along. And I'd best warn you that Lester Young has kin. They'll come after you for killing one of theirs. And one more thing you might want to know, I saw Lester Young deep in conversation with Tyler Bayfield before I came into the saloon.'

'I've a few things to do first,' Broke said. 'And then I'll take you up on your offer.'

Tander watched Broke head towards the general store and he went back to the saloon for a couple more beers. He couldn't quite make the man out. He reckoned he'd got lots to sort out for sure and hoped Broke wouldn't end up full of lead.

6

The buildings hadn't changed much in the years since Broke's abduction. The town had expanded back from Main Street, but those places he remembered were still the same.

As he peered into the gloomy interior of Graham Greenwich's General Stores, Broke imagined that even the cobwebs were the same ones he'd seen as a boy.

The store was the first port of call for all human needs, stocked with anything you'd wish to buy. As he looked about him he saw shelves where not an inch of space was wasted. The shelves were stacked high with everything from calico to canned oysters. The store supplied about everything to take the townsfolk from cradle to grave.

The odours wafting about the place were the same too, and still smelled of coffee, leather boots, pickled fish, dried meat and cotton fabric.

As Broke's eyes became accustomed to the dimness, they were drawn towards a pot-bellied stove at the centre of the store. A circle of chairs surrounded it but he'd expected to see men warming their feet as they chewed tobacco and drank coffee strong enough to break a spoon.

Usually, the place overflowed with customers and people who wanted somewhere to pass the time of day, but although the smell of the inhabitants, stale tobacco, burnt coffee and flatulence still drifted about, the place was empty.

The store was a place to exchange all the town news. It quickly dawned on him that they'd exchanged the latest gossip and that's why it was empty. Folks wanted to avoid him.

As he walked round the store and helped himself to the merchandise, his thoughts went back to the people he'd lived with for a long time. The Indians taught him survival skills that would see him through anything life could throw at him.

He hadn't planned to leave the Comanche, though he knew he would one day. It wasn't his natural environment but he'd been happy enough with his new family. 'The Beautiful but Barren Woman', the great warrior's wife, adopted him after the attack on his home. His destiny was to be a slave to the young Comanche braves.

His damaged leg, which had been almost severed by a lance, had saved him from a life of torture and toil. Beautiful, the name she used, admired his refusal to show any emotion, demonstrating, she said, his strength and courage. The only word he uttered to her was 'broke' as he pointed to his leg. So his name became 'Broke'. He refused to change it, even after his leg healed so well he wasn't left with a limp.

His position in the tribe, under her protection, became stronger — especially as she saw Broke as a good luck charm. Her name changed to 'Beautiful Mother of Twins' seven months later. He stayed for twelve years with the Comanche. However, when Beautiful died of fever, he decided to move on.

Broke put the memories aside. He needed to concentrate on what was required now.

He picked up a three button, pale-brown cotton shirt and a pair of dark brown wool pants. No one appeared to serve him, so Broke shucked off his old clothes in the middle of the store and replaced them all with the new ones. There were rows of shoes and boots and his gaze was drawn to a pair of black stovepipe boots. He pinched the leather to feel the softness between his fingers, and found that with some wool socks, the boots were his size. He'd thrown all his clothes into a barrel of wood by the stove, apart from his honey coloured buckskin coat, and his soft shoes. Moccasins were like a second skin, and if you didn't want to be heard moving around, they came in useful. He looked at the hats but decided he liked the neat bowler he always wore. And it fitted even better now he'd lost the hair.

Before he left he took one more thing — a Colt Frontier .44. Its hard rubber grip felt good in the palm of his hand. Its double action revolver allowed for rapid fire. Broke figured it was a gun he could get used to as he checked it over and placed it into the leather holster. The gun sat comfortably on his hip. He took a few hundred rounds of ammunition as well.

He walked out. There wasn't a storekeeper around to let know that he wasn't going to pay.

At the livery stables his attitude was just the same.

'I ain't sure you can do that, mister,' the stableman said. 'Tyler Bayfield wants cash up front before he'll let anyone touch the merchandise.'

Broke's hand ran over a saddle. It felt smooth under his palm. 'You tell my brother that this isn't even a down payment on what he owes me,' Broke said.

The stableman opened and closed his mouth, then stood and scratched his head. Clearly he had no idea how to handle this situation. What did he mean 'his brother'?

However he wasn't without a couple of brain cells. He watched as the man hauled the thirty-pound weight saddle on to his horse as if he was as strong as a buffalo. He scrutinized the man with the Colt Frontier nestling on his hip and the Henry rifle stowed into the new saddle and had second thoughts about challenging him. Family feuds ought to stay exactly there — in the family.

Yes sir, it wasn't his problem, he thought, he was only here to clear out the horse dung and stale hay.

7

When Broke and Gil Tander arrived at the Lazy Z Ranch, almost everyone was out after the wild ponies that grazed on the open range. In the late spring, the four-year-old ponies were rounded up to get ready to ride on the trail.

It gave Tander the opportunity to introduce Broke to Crosland Page, the man who owned the Lazy Z outfit.

Page wore a three-piece dark wool suit like he was ready to go to church and his face peered above the scratchy starched collar of a white shirt. Afterwards, Tander said his boss always dressed as if it was Sunday.

'This man says he's able to bust the horses for us, boss,' Tander said.

Page looked critically at Broke, 'I pay five dollars a horse. No more. Don't want anything fancy. Break them so the men can ride them.'

Broke nodded.

'That also gets you somewhere to sleep and chuck,' Page said. He turned to Tander, 'Show him where to bed down and stow his horse.'

Broke was dismissed. He wouldn't get any more attention until he proved he could do his job. That suited Broke. It had been a long day and it was far from over. They made sure their horses were settled and Tander pointed out where he could pitch his saddle. He put his guns with his saddle but his knife he kept tucked into his inside pocket of his jacket.

'Some sonovabitch stew here if you're hungry,' Tander said. 'Everything the cook produces tastes the same, so it don't matter what he calls it, we all know it's good ol' sonovabitch stew.'

Broke helped himself to a bowl. He nodded his head and agreed with Tander, but food was food and it filled the body so he wasn't about to complain. He had a second bowl. Since he'd left the Comanche tribe several days ago he'd had no thought or time for food.

'I think I hear the men coming back,' Tander said.

Distant cries of 'Hy-ar' came across the prairies and soon they saw a group of horses, raw broncos, flanked by a dozen riders. They swung round in a wide circle moving the horses towards the ranch. A spray of dust followed them as the galloping horses churned the dirt beneath their feet. Out of nowhere, men rushed to open the gates of the corral and twenty horses were trapped inside the large pen. A cowboy got off his horse and walked over to Tander and Broke.

'He's gonna break the horses, Hal,' Tander said.

This was enough of an introduction. The West wasn't a place where people stood on ceremony. A man did a job and that was it.

'Got everything you need in there,' Hal Smith said.

He pointed to a cow-saddle, bridle,

lariat, spurs, quirt and some short pieces of grass rope for the cross hobbling in the corner. Broke walked over and picked up a blanket from under the saddle.

'Don't need anything else,' he said.

His action and remark did attract attention.

'You sure he knows what he's doing, Tander?' a cowhand shouted.

Tander had watched Broke kill the gunslinger in the saloon, so quick he couldn't really say where the knife had come from. Tander nodded.

'He knows what he's doing.'

The men climbed on to the fence that surrounded the corral. All thoughts of food and rest and a drink of beer were gone.

'Sure you ain't brought a Comanche or a Kiowa back with you, Tander? 'Cause we ain't seen no white man walk into a corral full of wild horses without at least a whip.'

The remark sent a ripple of unease through the watching audience. It was a joky remark but said out loud it made them all feel uncomfortable. Trouble with Indians was sporadic, but neither race felt at ease with the other. A few homesteads had been attacked recently, by young braves incensed at being herded into reservations.

Broke concentrated on the horses, shaking with fear at their captivity. He could feel what they felt because he'd experienced it himself. One day you're running free, then it's taken away and life will never be the same again. He padded softly around the corral in the moccasins he'd slipped on again. He tried to make no sounds to disturb the horses.

They were an odd collection of wild mustangs. The blood of army horses and workhorses flowed through their veins. They'd roamed wild, feeding on the sparse prairie grass for about four years and were now old enough to be turned into horses suitable to ride the cattle trails.

Broke approached the biggest animal

and, though no more than twelve hands high, it had the look of a lead horse. Its nostrils flared in distress as Broke walked across to it. The horse reared and its hoofs looked ready to smash a man's skull.

'He's mad,' someone whispered.

No one else spoke. A couple of men swallowed as if their throats were dry. One man whispered they were all about to witness a man being crushed by a herd of wild horses. Then a raw sound, which afterwards the cowhands said was unlike anything they'd heard before, came from Broke's throat. The horse's hoofs came down but they didn't hit him. He held his hand out and reached for the horse's neck, all the time speaking in a language it seemed to understand.

Tander's heart thudded against his chest. He watched as Broke, with the same lightning speed as he'd seen him throw the knife, covered the horse's head with the blanket and swung on to its back. The horse, surprised at the move, galloped around the corral in utter panic. Again Broke spoke to the horse. No one could hear what he said, his lips moved but his voice wasn't audible to them. His hand wove into the horse's mane and he held on, legs tight round its girth.

Now the cowhands were certain the man in the corral was going to die. To them, there was no way a man could stay on a horse going that fast and exhibiting that amount of terror. Yet he wasn't thrown off. After two hours he dismounted and left the corral.

Broke knew that bronco breakers used tough measures. It was called breaking because the object was to break the horse's wild spirit through fear and lessons the horse would never forget. Hobbled, bridled and saddled they were ridden for over five days. The rougher the horse, the rougher the treatment he got, with quirts, spurs and ropes.

Every day the cowhands gathered to watch Broke. Bets were placed on how long it would take for the horse to tame the man. No one put any money on Broke taming the horse. Then on the fourth morning the horse trotted over to Broke. He saddled him up and rode him up to the main house of the Lazy Z Ranch. Crosland Page came out.

'You can put a child on this horse's back and it'll be as gentle as a kitten with them,' Broke said.

Page put his hand gingerly on the horse's neck. The horse turned and nudged him.

'You gonna take this long with every horse?' he asked.

The man wasn't about to give Broke credit for his work, but that was his way.

'No. Now the lead horse is tamed, the others will follow quickly.'

Broke turned and went back to the corral to continue his job. True to his word, the other horses were soon coming to his call, and willing to be saddled and ridden by the other cowhands. At first these cowhands had said they'd have a story to tell their children and grandchildren about the stupidity of a man. They did a quick rethink. There was a story to tell. And it would be about the bravery of a man who tamed horses without breaking their spirits.

Someone else watched as Broke tamed the horses. Lizbeth Page looked on in wonder as man and horse merged into one being. She gazed in fascination as one horse proved more difficult to control. All the other horses Broke tamed easily after he'd got the lead horse eating out of his hand. This one was unexpectedly proving to be the most wild. A beautiful beast, which except for its black socks and the mark that almost formed a dark star on its forehead, was pale grey.

Broke's body taut, he gripped its mane, and held on. The horse stampeded round the corral but it couldn't budge its load. Sweat dripped from Broke's body as he held tightly on to the horse. Its coat glistened with the effort of trying to shake him off. The girl observed and listened. She could hear the sound of Broke's voice, soft, soothing, whispering into the ear of the animal. The conflict went on for what seemed a long time. For short periods the horse became calm, but only to regain its strength to try and shake the rider off its back. Broke held on and never relaxed for a moment. On his face was written determination and a desire to master it.

Most watching would've bet a week's wages he'd not succeed in taming this one, and the horse would never answer to his voice and touch.

Then the tempo changed. No one could've said when it happened or if there was one thing that did it, but instead of fighting, the horse began to respond. There seemed to be a perfect accord between man and beast.

Broke heard the sound of muted clapping, as if to congratulate him for the end of a show. A beautiful young woman, hands clad in thin leather gloves, had seen and admired his skill and applauded him. He became aware of sky-blue eyes fringed with dark lashes and a face framed with ash-blonde curls.

'I didn't know we had someone who could break a horse by talking to it,' she said.

Broke climbed down to retrieve his hat. He brushed it over with his hand.

'Miss?' he enquired.

'Lizbeth,' she answered.

'Miss Lizbeth, you've got to stay on its back. No amount of talking will tame it otherwise.'

'But no whip and spurs? I've never seen it done without those before.'

'You don't have to kill its spirit to have a filly eating out of your hand, Miss Lizbeth,' he said.

'That's all very well, but surely it will only come to you? I suppose anyone else would be thrown in seconds of climbing on to its back.'

'Try it out,' he said. 'I guarantee your safety.'

Lizbeth Page, a girl known on the Lazy Z Ranch for her wilful spirit, jumped down from the fence to take up the challenge.

'Steady, Miss Lizbeth,' Tander warned. 'I don't think your pa would be pleased you getting on an untried horse.'

Lizbeth paid no attention.

'I think I can make up my own mind, Gil Tander,' she said. 'You just fuss too much about me.'

He had one last try.

'Broke, you can't let her do it.'

As the younger man shrugged his shoulders, Tander sighed.

'I know it's none of my business but how's the boss gonna take that explanation if his only daughter falls from the horse and breaks her bones?'

The Crosland Page he knew would probably sack half the hands and the other half he'd hang.

Tander turned towards the ranch house as Broke watched Lizbeth mount the horse. He was heard muttering that he knew whose bad books he'd prefer to be in.

The girl trotted round the corral so

she could try out the filly. The horse had been more scared than wilful and now displayed its good character. It was Lizbeth who showed the rebellious streak.

'Let's go for a ride.' She pulled the reins from Broke's loose grip, pressed her knees into the horse's sides and instructed a cowhand to open the gate. 'Only as far as Dead Man's Gulch,' she added.

Broke caught up with Lizbeth a few miles on. The horse, a muscular animal, had powerful hindquarters for sprinting. It galloped across the prairies, enjoying every moment of it.

'Turn back,' Broke ordered.

Lizbeth laughed and tried to spur the animal on. This time he didn't ask, he reached across and swung from his horse to hers. The horse, although now carrying an extra load, continued at an even pace. Broke brought the animal round well before they reached Dead Man's Gulch. It tested its mamoeuvrability as it turned effortlessly. It would make an excellent horse.

As they approached the Lazy Z Ranch it was obvious trouble waited for them both. Crosland Page was striding out from the ranch house with a bullwhip in his hand.

'Best disappear, Broke,' Lizbeth said.

She slipped off the horse and walked towards her pa.

'You'll be OK?' Broke asked.

He wouldn't leave her at the mercy of an angry father. It was his fault. He should've stopped her.

'Go on,' Lizbeth smiled. 'I can handle Pa.'

He only moved off with the two horses when he saw Lizbeth throw herself into her pa's arms. He knew he wouldn't receive the same kind of welcome. Chances were he'd have to keep out of Page's way until the man had time to calm down. He reckoned that if they came face to face too soon, the rancher would skin him alive.

8

Tyler Bayfield looked older than his thirty-one years. He was a large man and big enough to make a horse of fourteen hands look small beneath its load.

'Why that son-of-a-bitch kid couldn't have stayed dead, I don't know,' Tyler growled.

A lone coyote and a couple of prairie dogs pricked up their ears as he cursed 'til the air turned blue. It wouldn't change the way the whole doggone day had turned out but he had to let off steam or burst.

When Mitch Bayfield had turned up at the 3 Bay Ranch, Tyler thought he was a Comanche Indian. He'd fetched his gun, ready to blow the renegade's head off if there was any trouble. When he'd said he was a Bayfield, Tyler had frozen.

He followed his half-brother to Dead Man's Gulch and, perhaps too late in the day, took a few pot shots at him. If he'd been quicker witted he'd have shot him at the ranch. No one would have quibbled about the death of an Indian.

Then he trailed him all the way to town. Later he'd struck a deal with Lester Young, but the gunman fouled up the attempt to kill his half-brother.

He'd called in to see Marshal Jones. He wanted to know if there was anything he could do to get rid of Mitch because Tyler knew he'd want vengeance. If it had been him, he'd sure want to make someone pay for leaving him to grow up with those red devils.

Like his brother Mitch, Tyler was calling on a few debts. The marshal owed him. Everyone owed him. Tyler had bought up a lot of places in town. He always let the original owner run them but he had their profits in his hand. The Bayfield family prospered at everyone else's expense.

He'd kept Marshal Jones in an easy

job for years. He was the face of the law but he didn't really have anything to do with the running of the town. Like the stores, Tyler had bought the marshal, and he did as he was told. Any bad guys who showed their face in town got short shrift. One of the Young clan would enjoy some gunplay and get rid of them for the marshal. The Young clan always had enough shooting targets to keep them amused. That's how it worked. The marshal got a regular salary as well as a good pension to look forward to, with no risk to him.

It hadn't worked out that way tonight, because the fool Lester Young got himself killed. Tyler had always viewed Lester as a man with a ten-dollar Stetson on top of a five-cent head and he shouldn't have trusted him.

What he heard from Marshal Jones hadn't cheered him up any. In fact, it made him as unhappy as a pup that'd just had its tail docked twice.

'Can't you do anything to get rid of

him?' Tyler asked. 'He's a Comanche, in all but blood. Calls himself 'Broke'.'

The marshal shook his head.

'He's not a Comanche. You know, I know, the whole blame town knows that. And you know he's got work at the Lazy Z?'

Tyler couldn't believe Mitch was staying with Crosland Page. He'd had a quarrel with the man over land for years. He bit back his anger and didn't allow it to show.

'And you know he's killed a man,' Tyler said. 'That's reason enough to get rid of him.'

'Lester Young pulled a gun on him. There's a witness to say he was only defending himself.'

'Someone said Lester Young never got to fire a shot,' he said.

The marshal looked at Tyler Bayfield and frowned.

'That's the way it goes,' he said. 'The fastest man stays alive.'

Tyler persisted in reasons to get rid of him.

'The townsfolk say he's helped himself to everything he wants and not paid a cent for them.'

'You gonna get anyone to press charges? You for instance? You own most of the stores here.'

Tyler closed his eyes and a look of despair pervaded his features. Like the marshal said — as the owner of the stores, he wasn't going to charge his brother with thieving. A lot of grief could be stirred up taking that path.

'You go and shoot him, Marshal, the way you always do when a problem occurs,' Tyler said.

If Marshal Jones was forced to go after a bad man, he shot in the back and claimed they were resisting arrest. He said he figured you lived longer that way 'cause a town marshal often had a very short life span indeed.

This time, however, he refused to do as Tyler Bayfield ordered.

'A man rides into Hell, says he's a Bayfield, your half-brother, and ends up dead, don't you think people would ask questions about it?' he said. 'Or you got the judge and jury in your pocket as well?'

Then Tyler had an idea and a smile lit up his face.

'Let's see how well he does when the Young Clan go after him for killing one of their own,' he said.

It was nightfall before Tyler Bayfield finally made it back to the ranch. He visited the Youngs' homestead to tell them the bad news. It hadn't taken much to stir them up. As soon as their kin was laid in the ground, they planned to go after the Indian. Through the inky black of the night sky Tyler could see the glow from the remains of a cooking fire near the bunkhouse and small kerosene lamps burning in the window of the ranch. His father had probably gone to bed. He didn't do much nowadays; he just sat on the porch until it was time to retire to bed. Ever since he and Russell had returned home after the Indian attack to tell him Mitch was dead, he'd never been the same. He'd gone and looked for the boy for a while but hadn't found a trace.

Tyler swung his legs over the saddle and, as his feet hit the ground, one of the cowhands ran out to take the lathered horse to the stables. He knew, from the look on Tyler's face, not to ask if he was OK.

Tyler shucked off his wool jacket and walked into the ranch house. He took one look at his brother, clearly on yet another bender, and wrinkled his nose in disgust. Russell lay slumped against a chair, a whiskey bottle in his grasp.

He wore an incongruous outfit, dirty red flannel undergarments and a silk striped shirt. Tyler wondered if he'd started to dress and then the lure of whiskey interrupted the chore.

Long ago the two brothers began to detest each other. It hadn't happened overnight but if you tried to pinpoint the time their friendship cooled it could be said it was the time they left Mitch to die.

When Tyler suggested they give up

on Mitch, Russell hadn't exactly agreed but he'd gone along with the story that they'd looked everywhere for the boy and surmised that the Comanche had killed him like they'd killed his ma.

As far as Tyler was concerned it was an opportunity to get rid of the interloper. He hadn't been happy about his own ma getting replaced with indecent haste and, when a child came along, all he saw was another interloper with a share in the ranch. To his way of thinking, the Indian raid had done them a favour.

Russell, his younger brother, had slowly withdrawn into a shell where no one could reach him. Folks said he was grieving, but Tyler saw it for what it was, weakness and guilt. Every night in his dreams, he told Tyler, he cried because he could see Mitch calling out for help.

Whereas Russell sought the sanctity of madness, Tyler hardened, refusing to acknowledge there was more he could've done. One thing for sure, he hated Russell's lack of control just as his younger brother told him he loathed his lack of conscience. There wasn't a moment when the two weren't at each other's throats.

'How much more liquor you gonna tip down your gullet?'

Russell took no notice as he put the bottle to his lips and felt the fiery liquid soothe his throat. He'd given up using a glass. Took too much time to pour out a measure. Not as though he wasn't going to finish it all. Most mornings he woke up curled around an empty bottle as if it were a pretty woman.

Tyler's temper, even less contained than usual, spilled over as his brother ignored his question. Two steps brought him to where Russell sat sprawled out and his hands grabbed at the edges of the silk shirt and dragged him to his feet. He coughed and spluttered, but Tyler didn't care. The bottle fell from Russell's grip and smashed on the floor.

'What yer doing?' he protested.

Tyler shook him hard enough to turn him to jelly. Russell tried to grab the broken bottle, cut his hand in the attempt and saw blood mix with the yellow gold liquid.

'That was good stuff.'

His voice came out as a complaining whine. It varied from miserable to self-contempt. Tyler shoved the shards away impatiently with the toe of his black leather boot.

'Don't you care that Mitch Bayfield has turned up?' he asked.

Russell looked dazed. The news hadn't reached him because he'd been in an alcoholic stupor for most of the day.

Tyler pushed him back and sat him in a chair. There was no fight in the man. His brother would've been pleased to see a little bit of spark, which would give him an excuse to give his brother a whipping. For the moment, the pale eyes were blank.

The light from the fire highlighted the differences between the two brothers. Tyler, tall, imposing and considered a good catch by women, towered over Russell. Tyler had flourished in the wild untamed land whereas Russell, although born here, never seemed at home in America. His strong Irish roots gave him a fair skin, which burnt easily in the strong sun, red hair and a yearning for the Emerald Isles he'd never seen. At this moment, the call to visit his ma's homeland was strong.

Tyler took a fresh bottle, and two glasses, from the cupboard and sat opposite his brother. He poured two shots of liquor. As it went down, Tyler could understand why Russell sought to escape in its comforting arms. He put the stopper back on and ignored the frown Russell gave him.

'That was the last one,' he said. 'You've had enough. You are going to sober up and face what's coming.'

Russell's mouth shaped to form a protest but he didn't manage it. Tyler's fist found a good place to settle. Russell nearly ended up on the floor with the force of the blow.

'What you do that for?'

''Cause you asked for it,' Tyler said.

Russell's lip split and he tasted blood. His clothes now had dark red smears amongst a multitude of stains. But he didn't bother much with his appearance. Like his pa, he faced one day at a time and no more. In fact, according to his brother, the only time he washed was when he got caught out in a storm.

Tyler got on with brewing fresh coffee. He knew it would take a lot more than a pot to sober his brother up but it would be a start. The past had finally come to confront them and he and Russell had to show a united front. He began to pour pots of coffee into Russell's system. Russell pleaded to be left alone but Tyler, made of sterner stuff, ignored his brother. By the morning, Russell's pasty complexion, together with his red hair, gave him a clownish appearance — but he didn't reek of whiskey, and he wore a clean shirt and pants. Tyler had fed the wood stove with his old clothes and it had belched smoke in protest.

Now, if Mitch, or Broke — whatever he called himself — wanted to try and fill them full of lead, then they both needed to be ready.

9

'There's a gang of armed men riding in, Mr Page.'

The warning came from one of the cowhands.

Everyone appeared, with guns ready, at the man's cry of alarm. Crosland Page, shotgun in hand, walked on to the porch to meet the eight men who'd called, without invitation, to the Lazy Z Ranch. His gaze moved towards the one he considered was in charge — the man sat astride a horse that looked almost as mean as its rider. It snorted as the bit pulled at its mouth and the man slapped the quirt against its hindquarters. It didn't flinch.

'I've been told you got a feller working here who's responsible for killing my brother.'

'You got a name for yourself and 'this feller'?'

The mean-looking man stared hard for some sign Page meant to ridicule him. He found nothing. Everyone knew of the Young Clan. Over the years their reputation had grown.

'Name's Tom Young. These here are my brothers, Jared, Nuke, Cain and Bo, and my cousins, Luke, Jess and Pem.'

The Young Clan nodded as they were introduced. They were an odd assortment of men aged from about sixteen to fifty. All wore denim pants and homespun cotton shirts like a uniform of sorts. Every one of them, tooled up with a variety of irons, looked ready to round someone up for a lynching bee. This was confirmed by Tom Young's next words.

'I'm looking for a feller who looks a bit like an Injun. The marshal says he's that Mitch Bayfield boy who got took by the Comanche. I want him. We gonna hang him until he's dead — and some more.'

Only those close to Page would've noticed a slight tic at the corner of his mouth when the name Bayfield was mentioned.

'I don't know who this person is and I don't want any trouble on the Lazy Z Ranch. You look elsewhere and sort out your arguments away from my land,' he said.

He turned away and made to go in his ranch house but Tom Young called out to him.

'If I find he's hiding here, my friend, I'll be back to pay another visit. And you'll regret it if I do.'

The sound of rifles and guns being cocked ready to fire broke the stillness that followed Tom Young's words.

Page frowned.

'Nobody threatens me,' he said.

Surrounded by so many guns, Tom Young tempered his words. 'I over-reacted, friend. I'm sure you wouldn't hide such a bad man.' His crooked smile showed a mouthful of black teeth and rancid breath spilt out with his words. 'But if you see him, let me know.' He turned to his kin. 'Let's get outa here,' he commanded.

They followed his lead, and as one they forced their spurs into their horses' sides, and were off in a cloud of thick dust.

Broke watched as Tom Young and his kin rode out of the Lazy Z Ranch. He knew he'd have to deal with them. He couldn't risk being killed before he'd exacted his revenge on his brothers.

He was also keeping well away from Crosland Page.

According to Gil Tander, his boss was used to Lizbeth's antics and he'd soon simmer down. Broke thought with the Young Clan kicking up dirt, it might not be that soon.

He rode to Dead Man's Gulch, which he knew to be the best route between the prairies and town. And after living in the area as a kid, he knew everywhere well enough. To his left of the gulch was the land belonging to the 3 Bay Ranch, almost an adjunct to the Lazy Z, and to the right, the town.

He skirted round the area, and his

horse, fast as the wind, took him over the prairies to arrive just ahead of the Young Clan at the edge of Dead Man's Gulch.

Surprise flittered over Tom Young's face when he saw Broke sitting astride his horse his Henry rifle in his hands.

'I hear you're looking for me,' Broke said.

Tom Young's mouth puckered into an O, then he spat out a wad of tobacco before he choked on it. Quickly he composed himself as his red face settled to puce and he placed his hand on the lariat looped over the horn of his saddle.

'Marshal Jones didn't seem to want to deal with you when you killed one of my kinfolk, but we don't mind doing his job for him.'

'I took your brother out, fair and square,' Broke said. 'He drew on me first, but I was quicker than him with my knife.'

'So quick he didn't have time to fire his gun.'

Broke shrugged his shoulders.

'He didn't give me time to fire a gun either,' he said.

His gaze took in the eight riders and knew when he moved he'd have to make every shot count; he couldn't hesitate and remain alive. As he faced the men he had no time to wonder if he'd done the right thing.

Tander told him that often the Young Clan's style was to catch someone off-guard and shoot them in the back. Now they had their enemy face to face.

He calculated his chances. They were all killers, probably of differing abilities, but he'd have to treat them all the same, fast on the gun and dangerous.

Broke had fought alongside the Comanche, but only against other Indian tribes. He'd shot buffalo and game and within the tribe his skill with the gun, and knife, was second to none. He counted himself equal to the adversaries he now faced.

He counted on taking out four with his Henry rifle before they could get themselves together and react. The men who weren't quick enough ended up dead. These men though, Broke figured, would react faster than most. They looked as if they'd done their fair share of filling men's guts with lead.

'What are we waiting for, Brother?' Jared Young asked.

'We have plenty of time,' Tom Young replied. 'We can have some fun with this one. And from what I've heard, nobody is gonna ask what become of a Comanche who rode into town intent on trouble.'

Jared grinned wide enough to swallow a whole roast hog sideways. The laughter at Tom Young's comments echoed over the prairies and a circling hawk, startled by the noise, took flight and its wings beat a tune across the cloudless blue sky.

The Young Clan relaxed. They'd expected a real fight from a man who'd killed Lester Young. Initially disappointed because fighting brought colour to their mundane lives, they joked with each other about how enjoyable torturing him might be. If he screamed out when they 'roughed him up', no one would come to investigate because no one would care.

'Might be a reward somewhere,' Jared said. 'I hear the army will pay fifty dollars for every redskin's scalp. One less for them to kill I suppose.'

The colour of Broke's usually ice-blue eyes darkened with loathing as he listened to Jared Young. It was the white men who'd started scalping the Indians for the bounty paid and they in turn, believing that the soul would not go to the Hereafter without a scalp, took up the practice.

Broke followed every movement, every nuance, waiting for anything that would alert him to when they would make a move.

He didn't have to wait long.

'Let's hang him up,' Nuke Young said. 'There's a tree yonder.'

As Nuke's lariat spun into the air, Broke's hand was on the Henry rifle and firing. He fired four shots, each one taking a man out of the game. The bullets thudded into the chests of two of them, Nuke and Cain, and they toppled from their horses. A third bullet took the top of Bo's head off and for a moment he sat like he was trying to make out what had happened. The fourth bullet lodged in Jess's windpipe cutting off his cry for help before he too was dead.

As the firing stopped, and the gunpowder smoke cleared the air, Tom, Jared, Luke and Pem, the last of the Young Clan, saw that the man they were after had gone.

He'd disappeared right from under their noses.

'He can't have gone far,' Tom said.

The four horsemen stared hard as if this would bring back the man they wanted to kill to avenge their kin's death. The hawk's wing beats were long gone and it seemed the rest of the prairie creatures had vanished as well. It was so quiet that the whisper of the wind through the Ponderosa Pines and the spindly cottonwood trees sounded loud.

'He must be hiding in them trees,' Jared said. 'There's nowhere else to hide.'

Jared Young headed off towards the gulch. Luke and Pem didn't hesitate for a moment and went to follow him.

'Wait, you don't know what you're rushing into,' Tom shouted.

Luke and Pem took note of Tom Young and pulled hard on their horses' reins. After all, he'd got the right to be leader with all his experience and they were shook up by seeing four kin killed in front of their eyes. They'd all died, same as Lester, without having time to fire a bullet.

Jared, now a blur as he galloped into Dead Man's Gulch, crashed through the undergrowth like a man possessed. Then nothing.

A sound, like someone had forgot to grease the wagon wheels, came out of nowhere. It was a harsh noise that grated on the teeth and sent shudders down the spine.

The three remaining Young Clan looked at one another.

It could've been the noise which sent Broke's mount into action, but whatever startled the horse it reared up and sped off as if a snake had shook its rattle at it.

The Young Clan had no time to dwell on the incident. Tom, Pem and Luke barely had time to grab hold of the reins, as likewise their horses were spooked by the sudden noise, and galloped off to follow where Jared had gone a few minutes before.

They hadn't covered many yards when they were knocked off their horses and thrown hurtling to the ground.

10

Pem Young gagged as the roped tangled round his neck.

He always rode with his head low, believing this offered him protection. He said it was a way of avoiding stray bullets. He didn't make such a good target as those who sat upright. This time it wasn't the right move. A rope caught around his throat and he lay sprawled choking on the ground.

The other two, Tom and Luke, caught the rope across their chests and were momentarily left sitting in mid-air, bereft of horse and saddle, until they dropped with a thud to the ground. Their horses galloped on without them.

They guessed immediately who was responsible for unceremoniously tipping them off their mounts. The man they were after had strung a lariat across the trees to try and garrotte them. He'd turned the tables on them.

From the safety of his hiding place, Broke fired a shot at the foot of Tom Young's boot.

'Just follow your horses into town and we'll forget all about this,' he said.

'Tom, you ain't gonna let him get away with it?' Luke asked.

Tom Young agreed, as he watched Pem cough and spit blood-red sputum into his neckerchief. He ordered them to lie on their bellies in order to prevent the man with the gun getting a clear shot at them. His horse, along with the others, had gone with guns and ammunition. All they had were a couple of handguns between them but he was determined to make a good fight of it.

'We'll make an ordinary fight look like a prayer meeting,' he boasted. Inside he didn't feel so confident. But he couldn't let Pem and Luke know that. 'We're not moving from here. We're gonna get you. And when we do, we'll make you suffer and you'll beg us to kill you.'

He shouted across the clearing that

separated them. The bravado words were greeted with a shot near the toe of his other boot.

Broke laughed silently. The trick with the rope, to dismount his enemies, he'd seen the Comanche use. It proved effective. It levelled the battlefield and gave him some advantage. He had an armoury of weapons compared to them. Broke, with his brown shirt and pants, blended in well with the fallen leaves, undergrowth and the shadows of the trees. He could see what was left of the Young Clan clearly, with their grey white shirts, and they made a good target.

Although he hadn't planned this situation, years of living with the Indians had made him more in tune with nature and to the advantages of blending in with the scenery. He sat and waited for them to approach. He could see them crawling along on their bellies. He didn't wanted to kill them; they were nothing but a family trying to avenge one of their own. However, if they were determined to die he'd oblige, because they seemed intent on pursuing him. Broke waited, determined not to fire until he could see the fear curdling the whites of their eyes.

Four of their numbers were down, and one unaccounted for, but nothing stopped the Young Clan from pursuing their quarry. As they crawled along, Luke said he was sure he could see Jared. Tom saw him too.

'Keep going slowly,' he ordered.

Jared was propped against a Ponderosa tree. He looked like he was grinning. Closer to him, they could see his throat had been cut from ear to ear. He'd been scalped.

'Oh God!' Luke cried.

Tom Young's eyes were black, like the hatred in his soul for his brother's killer. His reason, like the hawk, had flown away. Lester Young had been heading for Boot Hill for a long time, but Tom, whose years should've given him wisdom, refused to see that would be his ultimate end.

'Take it easy,' Tom warned Luke and

Pem. 'We'll make him pay for what he's done.'

Waiting wasn't in Luke Young's nature. He got impatient and came running like a cub too young to know how to hunt. And Tom, who always acted like a grizzly bear towards the clan, couldn't move fast enough to stop Luke. He ran into the open, hollering and shooting, and made himself a target for anyone with a gun.

Broke watched for any movement. Sometimes the men were less visible as a dip in the terrain could make it seem as if the earth had swallowed them whole. The plains look flat to the uninitiated. Men familiar with the land knew the ground had hollows deep enough to hide a herd of buffalo. He wasn't about to go looking for them. Safely enveloped in the debris of the pine trees, its dead needles covering him, he waited. Then he saw a man run, shouting and shooting, at him.

Broke fired and brought him down with one shot.

'And here's me thinking you'd be in deep trouble and need a hand.'

Gil Tander, suspecting that Broke would challenge the Young Clan, had followed them. He'd taken a round-about route to avoid being spotted straight off. Tander didn't know too much about what had happened, but he'd seen the trick with the rope and was highly impressed. He'd also seen what had happened to Jared.

Broke's dark eyebrows came together in a frown. His voice low, he vented his irritation with Tander.

'Could've killed you, creeping up like that.'

Tander's mouth formed into a disparaging grimace.

'Take more than a greenhorn kid like you,' he whispered.

Broke's anger evaporated.

'They're almost at the edge of those pine trees,' he observed. 'They're determined to crawl into their own graves.'

'We can skirt round in a semi-circle and come up behind them,' Tander suggested. He smiled at the vision of the Young Clan's faces when they turned, saw them, and knew they'd been trapped. 'How many left?'

'Two,' Broke answered.

Tom and Pem Young noticed nothing until they heard the click of guns behind them.

'Drop your guns and get up nice and easy,' Tander said.

Hearing another voice, the Young Clan knew they were equally matched in numbers and outmanoeuvred, and had no choice. Slowly they got to their feet and turned to see Broke and Gil Tander.

'I never had a fight with you,' Broke said. 'Now just head back to town.'

Tom Young shook his head.

'You might have the upper hand on me now, but I won't rest until you are dead.'

Broke nodded. He could understand the need for revenge.

'Give them their guns, Tander, and we'll end this feud here,' he said.

Tander protested, 'I don't want to be part of a shoot-out.'

'It's not your fight,' Broke said.

'You gonna take on both of them?'

'Yes.'

Tander shook his head, then his gaze moved back to Broke's face and saw eyes, cold and cruel. He'd seen how fast the man could be with a knife. How would he match up with a gun? But he did what Broke wanted him to do. He watched the last two Young Clan, weapons at the ready, square up for a fight.

Pem Young fired his gun; his finger pulled the trigger fast. Broke was a split second slower but he was accurate. Pem's bullet went wild. Broke's Colt Frontier blasted lead and Pem Young dropped to his knees, a hole through his chest.

Broke fired again before Tom Young's bullet left the barrel. Tom went down with the force of a bullet between his eyes.

'Didn't take you long to kill eight

men,' Tander observed. 'I'd best send a wagon up here to pick up the bodies. I hope the marshal will believe it was self-defence again.'

Broke retrieved his knife from where Jared sat and wiped it clean across the dead man's chest. Then he reloaded the gun. It took a lot of bullets to kill all those men.

11

'You didn't play fair and honest with me, Gil Tander. You never owned he was a Bayfield. Get rid of him.'

Crosland Page's voice, together with the sound of his fist thumping the table, exploded across the plains. His daughter Lizbeth raised her eyebrows but didn't comment. She knew her pa would calm down faster if left to vent his rage. And she'd decided it was better to keep quiet after the incident of horse riding she'd indulged in yesterday. Tander wasn't doing anyone any favours by going against her pa.

'Boss,' Tander said trying to placate the rancher, 'I can vouch for him with the Young Clan. They came here looking for trouble. He gave them every chance but they wouldn't take it.'

'He's still a Bayfield.'

Page's belligerent voice boomed again.

Tander chose not to understand him.

'Look at the ten horses he's tamed. Taken him less than a week.'

'Bayfield,' Page growled.

'The man hasn't lived with the family since he was ten. He isn't responsible for what they get up to,' Tander said.

'No, it's even worse. He holed up with those savages.' Page was in a vindictive mood. 'Now explain the good in that since you're bent on defending him. And look how he disregarded the rules when it came to my daughter.'

'Well he didn't do anything against Miss Lizbeth's wishes,' he answered. 'You know she always does exactly what she wants.'

Lizbeth Page slunk lower in her chair and glared at Tander. She couldn't blame anyone. She'd acted like a hothead, but why harp on the subject?

Tander had worked for Crosland Page for years, from cowhand to foreman, and now virtually ran the ranch for his boss. Tander knew his word counted for something and although his boss made a lot of noise, he also knew he was a fair man.

'According to the story I heard, the young Mitch Bayfield got took by the Comanche as a slave after they killed his ma and burnt down the homestead. Folks say his brothers never liked his pa taking up with another woman after their ma died.' He paused as Page poured a beer and encouraged him to continue with the story. 'Somehow the boy and his ma were left alone when it was known there were raiding parties in the area. It's also said the brothers didn't spend too long looking for Mitch.'

Page's face creased with a grin. 'Tell him I want to speak to him. Even if he is a Bayfield.'

Broke stood in the large room that served as a place for eating and living, with rooms off to what he supposed would be a kitchen, and some bedrooms. He held his bowler hat in his hand, respectful of the fact the boss had invited him inside. He expected to be kicked off the Lazy Z Ranch but it didn't stop him from using his manners. He noticed the young woman sitting in a chair, next to a stove, darning some clothes. He nodded with his head towards her.

'I don't like your family,' Page said abruptly. 'Told that to Tander, and I'm stating that fact to you as well.'

If he'd expected a reaction he was disappointed. Only the small figure sitting in the corner let out a gasp of surprise. Broke looked at Page but held his tongue.

Tander had warned Broke about his boss's bad relationship with his folks on the neighbouring ranch. In fact, they'd darn well had what you'd call a range war ever since Page brought the land five years ago. The Bayfield family had decided it was theirs by right but hadn't even bothered to register the fact. They were so sure of themselves they had a shock when Page bought it from under their noses.

Broke didn't look as if it concerned him at all.

'You got nothing to say?' Page asked.

'I have my own quarrel with them. Don't need to discuss how I feel.

Page looked slightly taken aback. He'd expected something more from the son of his enemy. Then he reflected that the West wasn't a place for softness; that could be left to the women. He often said that, yet he knew his wife of twenty years, who'd moved here with him several years ago, had never complained about any hardships they suffered to get a better life. His daughter, Lizbeth, was the same. After her mother's death last year, she took her role as housekeeper and was as good a cowhand as any man. She was made out of the same stuff as most women who moved out west, tough as nails inside and gave as good as they got.

'That suits me,' Page said. 'But I like the way you work. Tamed those horses quicker than any man I know. Although I don't hold with you letting my daughter ride them.'

'It's not my job to control her. Needs someone more experienced than me.'

'I'd give you that job if it was possible to do it,' Page said.

Lizbeth threw down the mending and stamped out of the room.

'How about I offer to hire you? Finishing off the Young Clan shows you're a fighter,' he said. Before Broke could shake his head, Page continued. 'I got trouble. The ranch will go under if I don't do something. I've had more cattle rustled than anyone else round here. And now I've had a report that the Bayfield family, and a few others who'll do as they say, are fencing round all the land.'

Broke thought for a moment before replying, 'You'll always lose cattle. Got to be more vigilant. And you have to accept that cattlemen will fence what belongs to them.'

'At least investigate what's happening for me. Tander says you're the fastest man with a gun and a knife he's seen. And you've got the scouting skills of any Indian. I think I've had too many cattle stolen for it not to raise my suspicions that the 3 Bay Ranch might be involved. And I want you to make sure they're only fencing their land and not mine.'

'That's a lot you're asking,' Broke said. He could see the man needed help but he had other things on his mind and said so. 'I've a few scores to settle and then I mean to be on my way.'

'Name your price.'

'Ain't got a price,' Broke said. 'But OK, I'll take a look-see before I move on.'

12

Marshal Jones waited outside the Lazy Z ranch house with his shotgun for Broke to step outside.

'I'm arresting you for the murders of the Young Clan,' he said. Marshal Jones's gaze also took in Tander. 'And you ain't gonna be able to defend him this time. One man in a saloon might be overlooked but this . . . you've killed eight men. Almost ran outa fingers counting the dead bodies arriving in town.'

'Those men came chasing after him,' Tander said. He ignored the marshal's words. 'Broke was only one gun against eight.'

'So you saw it all? Again? You can vouch it was self-defence?'

'Well, it was almost over when I got there,' Tander explained. His voice tailed off with the look on the marshal's face.

'And you got nothing to say?' Marshal Jones aimed his words at Broke.

Broke stared blankly at the marshal. He felt there weren't any words possible when you've already been tried and found guilty.

'Let's get back to town,' the marshal said.

Tander's hand moved towards to his gun. Broke stopped him with a few words.

'This is my business,' he said.

Broke noticed people's reactions to him right from the start. He made them feel uncomfortable. He was a man that made them face up to the fact they'd betrayed him. And he wasn't one of them. Not now. The Comanche tribe had brought him up and that made him an outsider. The people in town had no time for him. If they had doubts about the wisdom of locking the man up it wasn't said in words. The way they turned away made it clear they'd washed their hands of the man, just as they had the boy.

He sat in the silence of the adobe prison. Of all the buildings, this place was the sturdiest in Hell. A wry smile played over his face. Perhaps it was fitting that this was the end of the line. Incarcerated in Hell.

He wasn't the type to give up and in the next hour he examined the room the marshal had locked him in. It was strong but every place, he reasoned, same as every person, has a weakness. He found it in the narrow barred window. It would be a tight fit but he'd decided he wasn't going to stay around for his appointment with the hangman.

Maisy Martin also decided that Broke shouldn't hang. She was the woman he'd told to leave town. After a good deal of cussing at his boldness, she'd taken his words as well meant. Why shouldn't she leave and start again? As she waited for the stagecoach to take her away from this place, she'd seen the marshal ride into town with Broke in tow. She knew she couldn't leave with Broke in trouble.

The deputy marshal let her in. Deputy Don Wills didn't see her as the saloon girl. Now dressed in a plain dark-blue dress and bonnet, he treated her like a lady. She smiled at him.

'I'm from the church,' she said. 'I just baked a cake and thought the prisoner might like a piece.'

It had been a long time since she'd been inside a church. It hadn't figured in her life as a saloon girl and it would take her a long time to confess everything. But perhaps God would look on her kindly if she helped a friend.

'You ain't got no gun baked in that cake?' the deputy asked.

Maisy Martin gave him a withering look and the joky comments died on his lips. She hoped he didn't insist on looking in her basket — while there was food and water for her journey out of Texas, there was nothing resembling a cake.

'Sorry, ma'am.'

'No that's all right, Deputy. You have to be careful. We ladies from the church think it's our duty to help these poor unfortunates. We ask God to forgive them before they hang.'

'Don't waste your time on him, ma'am. He's a savage. Lived with the Comanche for too long. He's killed more men than I've had hot dinners since he came to town a few days ago. Have to lock up animals like that.' Deputy Wills tapped the keys on his belt. 'I'm here to make sure he don't escape.'

'You don't say? You must be so brave,' she said.

Pleased to have an adoring audience, Wills — young, spotty and naïve — blushed and offered Maisy Martin a chair to sit on.

'You want a drink of coffee? If that's not too strong a brew of course.'

'That'll suit me fine.' Maisy blinked coyly at the youngster, 'Your ma must be proud to have such a helpful son.'

The young deputy stuttered a reply

as he filled a large mug and a small cup with coffee, 'Well my ma don't think as generously as you, ma'am. She reckons the place I keep my brains wouldn't make a drinkin' cup for a canary.'

'Surely not,' Maisy Martin said. With a deft slight of hand, practised and more suited to a card table, she slipped a very large drop of laudanum into his coffee. 'She must be joshing you.'

'My ma don't josh no one, ma'am,' he said.

The deputy relaxed as he made conversation with the lady. He wasn't too happy about guarding this prisoner but she made the time pass pleasantly. He got through three mugs of coffee as they sat there together. He gave a big yawn and turned red with embarrassment.

'Excuse me.'

'You'd best have another coffee,' Maisy said. 'Help keep you awake.'

'I think I'll do that . . . '

Deputy Wills crashed on to the floor. Maisy hastily took his keys. She went through the door to where the cells were. Broke stood up as she entered the rear of the marshal's office.

'Pay back time?' Broke asked. 'You gonna pray for me before I hang?'

'I ain't here to gloat.' Maisy opened the door to his cell. 'Better get out fast. That deputy's snoring is so loud that soon the town will think thunder is rumbling across the prairies. Already sounds like a hog being fetched for slaughter.'

'You're taking a risk,' Broke said.

'No risk. He ain't gonna wake up for at least half a day, put enough laudanum in his coffee to see to that, and he'll not remember a thing,' she said.

Broke stepped out of the cell, checked that the man was out cold, and then looked at the woman.

'You're not going to keep any friends doing that in this town,' he said.

'I've no intention of staying long enough to worry about that,' she said. 'The next stagecoach leaves within the hour and I'll be on it. You did me a favour. In fact, it's a pity you didn't come along a few years earlier.'

Broke's normally unreadable face pulled into something that might pass as a smile.

'You'd have beaten my britches if I had,' he said. 'Only twenty-three summers have passed since I was born.'

Her eyebrows rose questioningly at the turn of phrase.

'Do you think you're ready to leave the only real people you've known?'

'Like you, I have to move on,' he said.

He didn't explain further. He'd made a decision and there wasn't anything to discuss. Maisy Martin shrugged her shoulders.

'Yes I suppose you do, so I wish you luck,' she said. 'I don't think anyone is going to chase after you. Most people thought Marshal Jones a fool for bringing you in.' Her voice lowered a couple of octaves and she whispered her next words. 'Folks know that he did what your half-brother Tyler told him to do. Those boys don't want you around now, anymore than they did all those years ago.'

'You sure Marshal Jones is gonna let me walk out of town?'

'As I said, Marshal Jones has done what Tyler asked him. Brought you in, but perhaps Tyler didn't specify he had to keep you in.'

'And the townsfolk?' Broke asked. 'Why should they want to be reminded about a boy they left to rot?'

'You have every right to be angry, but don't let it eat your soul,' Maisy said. 'I'm as wicked as the other townsfolk. I knew your ma before I turned bad and I should've cared to what happened to her son as well. But I can't change things now.'

Broke's face had gone back to being impassive. She was speaking of things that could've hurt a lesser man. She reached up and put a hand on his shoulder. He didn't flinch, but then he didn't react at all.

'Thank you for telling me to get out of Hell. I'm going to a town a lot further away. And you know, I'm going to be the widow woman I should've been a long time ago.' She picked up her basket. 'Sorry I couldn't manage a cake but help yourself to the marshal's armoury.' She pointed to the deputy's keys. 'Should find a Colt or a rifle to suit.'

'Thanks, Mrs Martin,' he said.

As she reached the door she turned and looked back at him, 'Broke, or Mitch Bayfield, whatever you're called, don't make the same mistake as me and stay too long in Hell.'

As Maisy Martin had predicted, folks let him ride out on the horse that had brought him into town. However, this time there was no marshal with a gun pointed to his head, and his hands weren't roped to the horn of the saddle. The townsfolk turned their heads away again as if they didn't notice him.

It seemed like no one wanted to try a man for getting rid of an unsavoury bunch of vagabonds who thought nothing of shooting the town up for the fun of it. And who would relish the idea of punishing a man who had already been a captive for committing no crime at all?

As he rode out he noticed all these things. It was in his mind to wonder if Maisy Martin was right about the marshal and the sore-headed deputy. Would they be pleased he'd got out of jail? Then he pushed the thoughts away. He wanted a clear head. He had a job to do for Crosland Page's Lazy Z Ranch and he reckoned he'd be able to settle the score with his two brothers at the same time.

Deep in thought, he barely noticed a rider going as fast as the devil, and coming after him.

13

Folks living around Hell, homesteaders on the prairies had suffered from Indian attacks over the past few months.

Sanda Hutting had watched helplessly as a group of Indians killed her husband and three sons and then set fire to the house. Forest, her seven-year-old son, had been wrenched from her grasp, and taken away. The renegade laughed as Sanda screamed and cried at the loss of her child.

It took her a while to get free of the bonds that tied her, crawling across the ground until she found something, an old axe blade, to saw through the ropes round her wrists.

As soon as she was free, she walked the five miles to town.

It was hard to leave the bodies where they lay but her thoughts centred on her one live son. She wondered how long they'd let him live after they'd had their fun. She arrived in town after Marshal Jones had locked Broke in the jail. She went into the marshal's office to ask for help.

'Had my fill of Injuns lately,' he said.

'I need help to find Forest, Marshal,' she said.

Marshal Jones's gruff manner surfaced and spilt over.

'Got more than enough to do,' he said. 'You folks, you come out here, well you should know the risks.'

Fortunately Sanda Hutting, made of stern stuff, didn't keel over in a faint, or cry. She stood her ground and asked for help again.

'When we moved here I heard a rumour that this town doesn't help its own,' she said, 'but I couldn't believe it to be true.'

'The army is the one to ask. It's not my jurisdiction. For now, go over to Second Street to the undertaker, Jan Coots. Bury your kin and go back East.'

'Lived here eight years, Marshal

Jones, I ain't got family other than around here,' she said. 'That is, the family that's left is in the hands of the Injuns, but from what you're saying it looks as if I'd best go look myself.'

Outside the door of the marshal's office, Sanda Hutting refused to allow a tear to escape. She sniffed hard and took off to the undertakers to sort out the practical things.

Jan Coots, carpenter, coffin maker and undertaker rolled into one, knelt on a box and hammered nails as fast as he could. He looked up when Sanda Hutting came in the yard then spat nails from his mouth before saying hello.

'Take a seat, Mrs Hutting. You look as if you could do with a cup of strong coffee. If you were a man I'd offer to pour a drop of my coffin varnish in it.' Sanda's eyebrows rose quizzically. Jan explained, 'Just a drop of whiskey, I meant.'

'Don't let anything stop you doing right that, Mr Coots,' Sanda Hutting said. 'I've been through as much as any man I know.'

Jan Coots didn't ask what troubled the woman. She'd say when she was ready. He looked darkly at the number of coffins he had to make.

'At this rate I'll be taking on someone to assist me 'cause I can't manage all this work myself.'

Sanda looked at the four coffins standing against the wall and the pile of wood stacked up to make more. While she waited for him to brew a pot, she forgot her own troubles for the moment and asked him how come he was so busy.

'What happened?' she queried.

'A man, name of Broke, he says, comes into town and starts shooting. That's what happened. Next dang thing I know — sorry, ma'am, it's been a busy time — anyhow next thing is, I'm making coffins for the whole of the Young Clan. He ain't been the cause of your woe, has he?'

A sob escaped her throat and Jan

Coots waited for the tears to flow but Sanda Hutting held her weeping back. It wasn't time to be weak, she told Jan.

'We got raided by Injuns. Killed my family, all but my boy, and they took him.'

'Count yourself lucky then. If he'd come after you then there'd be no one left to tell the tale.'

'Who is this man? Won't the marshal lock him up?'

'Well he's locked up now, but no one wants him to come to trial.' He stood up straight, flexed his back to ease the pain from all the sawing and hammering he'd done. 'Similar circumstances to you, ma'am, this man's family, that is his ma, got attacked by Comanche, she got killed and he got took off. Now he's back and he's got a head sore as a bear woken early from his winter sleep.'

'I still don't see why he'll not be brought to justice,' Sanda Hutting said.

Jan Coots handed her a coffee, strong enough to float a log on it, with the 'varnish' to sweeten it.

'Broke, who used to be called Mitch Bayfield, reminds folks of the past. They want him gone, but not because they'll hang him. That way he'd never leave. His ghost would walk the streets of Hell on earth.'

The undertaker went on to tell her the story of how the father and two older sons went to town for supplies and when they got back there was nothing but a funeral pile.

'Wasn't much left to bury of the woman and there was no sign of the youngster.' Jan sat down, balancing precariously on some planks of wood. 'There was a half-hearted attempt to find him by the brothers, but in the end no one found anything to say if he was dead or alive.'

'And now he's back to settle some scores?'

'That about sums it up, Mrs Hutting.' Jan Coots drained the dregs from his cup. 'Now if you're feeling better I'll get someone to go with you with a wagon and get those bodies, I mean, your folks, and I'll give them a decent burial.'

'Thank you, Mr Coots,' she said. She stood up and looked towards the door. She guessed she couldn't keep the man from his work any longer but she lingered long enough to ask, 'How come no one helped the family?'

'That's not strictly true. People rallied round and cleared the site so the Bayfield family could start rebuilding their home, but everyone was under attack by the Injuns, far worse than the odd renegade shooting up a homestead, begging your pardon, and they had to defend themselves.'

Jan Coots took up a hammer and banged it down on a nail. He wasn't usually so talkative but the atmosphere was tense and it'd welled up inside 'til he got it off his chest. He reckoned he'd said enough words to last him a lifetime.

There'd been a hornet's nest stirred up to fury by Broke's arrival and it had made everyone think about what they could've done to help. To Jan Coot's way of thinking it was fruitless to go over the past. It changed nothing.

'I'm sure you're right, Mr Coots. You can't change the past, but you can learn a few lessons from it.'

Sanda Hutting wasn't one to believe in fate. There were many paths to choose in life. You could steal food or plant crops. You could pull a gun or live peaceful with folks. People were able to decide these things. She was going to try and alter the future. As she picked up the hem of her skirt and ran back towards the marshal's office, she decided that Forest wasn't going to live the rest of his childhood as an Indian boy.

In the hour that she'd spent talking to Jan Coots, Broke had been left with Deputy Marshal Don Wills and escaped.

She also found out that townsfolk had watched, glad to see him leave. She wasn't about to watch her last hope leave and, without a moments thought about the consequences, she unhitched a horse from the rail along the marshal's office and rode as if all those people in Hell were after her.

'You've got to help me!'

As the rider reined level with his horse, Broke's gaze took in a small dark-haired woman about thirty. She wore a torn, homespun dress. His hand hovered over the Colt Frontier he'd retrieved from the marshal's office. He hadn't seen her before and he didn't know her.

'What do you want, ma'am?' he asked.

She looked as if she was fighting for breath. It was evident she'd ridden hard; her horse, all lathered up, shook its head and spitballs flew from its mouth. Her face streaked with dirt, eyes glistened with tears, but she had an inner strength that shone through the mask of desperation covering her face. For a few moments she couldn't speak. He waited patiently.

'I'm Sanda Hutting. Everything I have is gone.'

The words, uttered through lips drawn hard and thin, were spoken quietly.

'Can I take you anywhere?' Broke asked. 'You want to go home?' When he saw the look that came upon her face, he added quickly, 'Perhaps you'd come to the Lazy Z Ranch with me. Miss Lizbeth Page could help you out.'

'The Injuns raided our homestead yesterday. They burnt it down. They killed everyone except me and my boy.' Broke saw her swallow hard before she went on. 'They left me alive because they seemed to enjoy watching me scream and plead for mercy when they took my son.'

The picture of his past came strong into Broke's mind. He could smell smoke. He could taste blood. He could feel the horror of being snatched from his home.

'I'll take you to Lazy Z Ranch. They'll look after you,' he said.

The woman looked at Broke.

'And you'll help get my boy back?'

she asked. 'You lived with Injuns all those years. They'll listen to you. You're one of them.'

Her eyes searched for anything on his impassive face that would let her know what he'd do. Hope died on her face as he spoke again.

'I'll give you the same help this town gave me all those years ago,' he said.

Lizbeth, as Broke promised, took the woman, Sanda Hutting into the ranch house.

'Aren't you gonna help her? Her son, Forest, he's the only kin she got left,' Tander pleaded.

'No,' Broke answered.

14

Broke noted the look of surprise on Gil Tander's face but he turned away and rode out of the Lazy Z Ranch.

In his mind he mulled over the past, when the Comanche had taken him. It had affected him more deeply than he'd believed.

He hadn't quite left the Comanche ways behind. He had a few arrowheads and a length of sinew with him. He found a suitable Osage tree and carved himself a bow stave. Soon he had a useful weapon hung across his back. He used his knife to slit the throat of the first deer he brought down with an arrow. The second he killed outright.

The Comanche people, after waging a war lasting forty years, had finally moved to a reservation between the Washita and Red River. The land was to the east of the Lazy Z Ranch near the

Goodnight-Loving cattle trail.

It was to this place that Broke headed.

He hauled the two deer, lashed to a travois, behind his horse, as he entered the reservation. People stopped whatever they were doing and stared at him as he rode in, approached his adopted father's tipi and asked to converse with him. Fighting Bear wasn't only a great warrior, but he was held in great respect because of his twin sons, given to him at a great age by his youngest wife.

Broke noticed the angry stance of the young male braves and saw women look away from him, their eyes downcast. Everywhere he saw mistrust written on the faces of the people. Only one woman, Little Bluestem, named because of the unusual colour of her eyes, stared at him.

His adopted mother's eldest twin son, known as Black Horse, and now thirteen years old, came out and greeted Broke. He was learning the mantle of responsibility, as his father grew old. Black Horse was near to the age when he 'made his medicine', a rite of passage in which he would be recognized as a man.

Broke and Black Horse had lived as brothers. Broke sensed that the death of Beautiful, together with him leaving the Comanche, had caused a crack in the fabric of their relationship. Nevertheless, Broke played on their friendship and reminded Black Horse of the many good times they'd shared together.

Broke also showed his respect towards Wolf Slayer, Black Horse's younger brother by one hour. He offered the two deer he killed with his bow and arrows as a feast to them and all their people. As a thank you, he was invited to eat with the tribe. Broke knew he was in for a long stay. He'd warned Tander not to expect him back for a day or two.

A feast was an important ceremony.

Such was the Comanche way of life that they feasted when food was plenty. Fresh meat couldn't be kept long and they'd rather a full belly, than be frugal. Then they'd have a lean time when game was not so available.

The women cooked while the men smoked and talked. It was the way. Men hunted and women collected, prepared and cooked the food. All had a place in the tribe. Life was hard for both men and women.

The feasting was well underway before Broke could speak about what had brought him to the camp. The Comanche had no love of palefaces, whom they considered the destroyers of their land. They killed buffalo and then herded a proud people into reservation lands where they expected nomadic bands of people to farm. Broke had lived with them for too long to believe it would work out, because he couldn't see hunters being turned into farmers.

They sat together round the fire and its light flickered over their bodies. The younger men had painted their faces and bare chests; under the glare of the flames they looked fierce and angry. Violence curled up inside, ready to spill out. Broke knew they were the braves who were raiding the homesteads. They were painted to frighten their enemies.

Broke held out a calumet towards Fighting Bear. Its beautifully decorated soft stone pipe bowl drew admiration from the onlookers.

'A gift for you,' Broke said.

He handed the pipe to the Fighting Bear together with some kinnikinnick, a mixture of tobacco and herbs, to smoke.

To his two Comanche brothers, Black Horse and Wolf Slayer, he offered knives with handles of buffalo horn, one carved into the shape of a horse, the other, a wolf. He fashioned the knives last year to present them when they'd become recognized as great warriors. He knew this was a good a time as any to hand out presents.

Only when they had all passed the pipe around did he explain the reasons for the visit.

'The Lazy Z Ranch is growing bigger,' he said.

A lofty young brave, He Who Would Grow Tall As A Mountain, jumped up in rage.

'You think we don't know this? That this rancher's stock is straying into our reservation?'

'It doesn't take long for the palefaces to take the little they have given us,' Wolf Slayer said.

'I agree with you that something has to be done,' Broke said. 'The Lazy Z Ranch has also been losing some of its stock.'

'And we have lost nearly all of our stock of buffalo,' Fighting Bear said.

Impetuous young voices gave vent to their rage, 'We ought to kill all of their cattle to make things even. Kill the palefaces.'

Round the fire, a few older heads than theirs nodded in agreement.

'They have more cattle to replace them with,' Broke said. 'And if you kill the palefaces the army would return. No matter how many you kill more will come.'

'Why have you come here?' Black Horse asked. 'Are you accusing us of stealing the Lazy Z cattle?'

'I do not accuse you of anything. The

130

ranchers are fighting because they need more land. I have a proposition to put to you.'

He waited for his words to be accepted. The atmosphere round the fire was tense. Things could go either way, he would be allowed to continue to speak or he'd be banished from the campfire or worse.

'So what do you want to say to us?' Fighting Bear finally asked.

'I can make sure you are supplied with cattle for free,' Broke said.

There was momentarily silence round the camp-fire then uproar.

'We cannot steal but you can give them to us for free. You can give us cattle that aren't even yours? Which hat do you wear? Living amongst your own kind for a short time has addled your brain,' Thunder River said.

'Lazy Z Ranch needs to expand. He needs a good space near the paleface's cattle trail. I have seen your reservation. It isn't farmland. There are many, many unused acres.' Broke paused as he saw

Thunder River's hand go towards his tomahawk.

'Are you suggesting that they take this as well?'

A lesser man might have feared for his life. Broke faced him out.

'No,' he said. 'This is yours. The paleface wants more land. Rent it back to him. Take his money. Let his cattle graze here. You'll have what you need to feed yourself right here.'

'Ignore what he says,' He Who Would Grow Tall As A Mountain growled. 'Let's continue to kill the homesteaders, ranchers, cattle, anything that comes on to our lands.'

'You will lose everything if you do these things,' Broke warned.

Although Broke had made sensible suggestions, he knew it would take a while for them to be accepted. Nothing could be agreed without discussion. And he wouldn't be part of that. He hoped they might go along with his idea because, at the moment, he had some standing with the Comanche people.

Fighting Bear and the other elders of the tribe had to win over young braves who wanted to continue fighting.

The Comanche were made up of many violent, warring bands but they respected strength and the fact that this band knew him well, was the reason they allowed Broke to sit with them. From the moment they'd captured him as a boy he'd shown he had strength in mind and body. Added to that, everyone adored his adoptive mother, the great warrior's wife, Beautiful Mother Of Twin Sons — and she had given him status.

Broke took his leave, but before he left the reservation he pushed his position within the tribe to its limits.

'You have a boy here,' he said. He looked deep into the eyes of his adopted father, Fighting Bear and the twin Comanche brothers. He stared right down to their very souls, and pleaded with them. 'This boy is paleface. Forest Hutting. Allow him to go back to his own kind.'

'You lived with us as a boy,' Wolf Slayer said.

'Yes, and now, as a man, I belong nowhere,' Broke said.

'What can you offer in exchange for the boy?' Black Horse asked.

Broke had nothing.

He considered what they might regard as a prize.

'My scalp.'

There was silence.

Then Fighting Bear, Wolf Slayer and Bear Follower rocked with howls of laughter. The Comanche were proud of their long hair, which they rarely cut and decorated with cloth, beads and feathers.

'What would we want with that? You're almost bald!' Black Horse said.

'You look worse than the Big Cannibal Owl we use to frighten the naughty young children,' Wolf Slayer laughed.

15

Joe Vincent stretched his arms upwards as far as they'd go.

It eased his back pain. In his opinion he was getting too old for cow work. It was a young man's life, out in all weather, getting your legs gored by cows that didn't have the sense to know which way to go. He was fed up with eating food off a chuck wagon, poor victuals that either gummed a body up or produced enough wind to blow all the cattle across Texas to Chicago.

Now he was hammering wood posts into the ground because he'd been told to fence off the land owned by the Bayfield family. He took his orders from Tyler Bayfield, the elder of the Bayfield brothers. Russell agreed to whatever Tyler decided, which made it easier for Vincent, because having two bosses didn't work. He never included Kit Bayfield, who actually owned the 3 Bay Ranch, because long ago the old man had handed over the reins to his sons through lack of interest in anything or anybody.

Word was that after his wife and son died he'd lost the will to live and merely existed. Whether that was true, Vincent had no idea. He hadn't been around then, he'd travelled all over the country doing work wherever it was found. He was content to earn his dollar a day and spend his greenbacks in town at the end of the month.

The job they'd asked him to do now made him feel uncomfortable. He could work as hard as the next man, it made payday come round a bit quicker, but all this fencing off land spelt trouble and he wasn't happy. The wagon, full of wooden posts and barbed wire, moved slowly along the boundaries of the ranch. Every few yards it'd stop and another post would be driven in and wire run from one to the other.

'How far is this gonna go, Joe?' Sid Nevit asked.

The cowhands hated fences because, used to roaming free across the prairies, the whole idea of fencing the place off stank of trouble. Vincent knew Tyler Bayfield wanted a fight with the Lazy Z Ranch. It was an excuse to get rid of Crosland Page and get more land.

'We're taking it as far as the eye can see because the boss reckons it's the finest fencing in the world. It's as light as air, stronger than whiskey, and cheaper than dirt. Or so the salesman told him,' Vincent laughed. 'We're to fence the Lazy Z Ranch land as well.'

Nevit whistled through a mouth missing too many teeth to look pretty, and a sound like a cat swallowing a canary came out. He shook his head but, like the rest, he just followed orders and didn't make any objections. However his face said it all.

'I know, Sid,' Vincent said. 'I don't like it anymore than you do. If we go against Bayfield we'll end up without a job. Maybe worse.'

The Bayfield brothers were disliked

by most people roundabout and fencing off land wouldn't increase their popularity. So Vincent and the other cowhands got on with the job. Sweat poured off them as the sun beat down. Occasionally they paused long enough to take a drink from the water bottle that got passed round, but mostly they worked. At the 3 Bay Ranch no one stopped until nightfall, or until a job was done.

A few hours, and many posts and yards of barbed wire later, Tyler Bayfield rode out to inspect their progress.

'Good work, men,' he said.

Vincent looked up from stretching the barbed wire, which even though he wore thick leather gloves, had managed to bite into the flesh of his hands. His boss was mean when it came to giving a good word to anyone and it surprised him. He watched Tyler Bayfield's lips settle into a satisfied happy grin. Normally the man snarled ugly enough to frighten a dog off a gut wagon.

'Crosland Page ain't gonna like this boss,' Vincent said.

'That's what I'm counting on.'

Tyler Bayfield's smile broadened as he pulled his hat further down his forehead to shield his face from the sun. Sweat trickled down the back of his neck but if his men thought he'd tell them to take a break because of the heat, they were disappointed with his next words.

'Don't take too long with this fencing,' he said. 'Quicker it's done, quicker you can call it a day.'

'Take more than a day, boss,' Vincent volunteered.

'That's why I told you to take some food and sleeping gear out with you. Don't anybody come back until it's finished.' He clicked his tongue and pulled slightly too hard on his horse's bit to turn it towards the ranch. 'I'm off. Dang well too hot for me out here.'

The cowhands silently watched Tyler Bayfield ride off. As far as Vincent was concerned, they'd got the last laugh, because even with the heavy workload foisted on them, none had a devil on their back like Tyler and Russell. Both brothers were tooled up with extra irons; in fact they looked like they'd given the gunsmith his best business for a long time.

Talk at the ranch, and in town, so some of the boys said to Vincent, was that the Bayfields' brother was back from the dead and was after pumping them full of lead. A lot thought they deserved it and had it coming for a long time. The Bayfield family hadn't tried to integrate themselves one little bit. Kit Bayfield, now a virtual recluse, allowed his two sons full rein. The pair, especially Tyler, were considered bullies and had moved from beating up smaller kids to taking over the town.

Tyler Bayfield was the one people answered to, his brother Russell followed his lead. He was an astute businessman who bought up people's debts and they paid him plus extra interest. If they couldn't, he'd take over completely and put someone in to manage the place. Over the last few years he built a small empire in Hell. It was also Tyler who'd built up the ranch; hence the fight with Crosland Page when he discovered the man had already bought up the extra acres of land he'd eyed up as his next purchase. And it was this land he was fencing off now.

Tyler returned to the ranch, after inspecting the fencing, feeling good about the situation and sure that he was going to get the upper hand with Crosland Page. The feeling didn't last. A couple of nights later Vincent came to the ranch with bad news. Someone was bent on destroying the fences. Tyler and Russell rode out to inspect the damage.

'Sorry, boss.'

Vincent apologized as if he'd been the one to cut the barbed wire. Tyler pulled his horse so hard it kicked up on its front hoofs, protesting at the abrupt stop. Tyler lashed his quirt across its haunches.

'What on earth . . . ?'

As far as the eye could see the barbed

wire fence, carefully placed there the day before in two neat rows across from one post to the other, had been cut so effectively, they'd have to buy new wire. Tyler walked back and forth along the length of the destruction. He fumed and cursed.

'I think it's the work of Injuns.'

Vincent volunteered the information without realizing he was treading on delicate ground. He'd forgotten Tyler's brother had spent half his life with Indians and the man had taken up with Crosland Page. It shouldn't have been a shock when Tyler Bayfield lifted his quirt again and hit out to give the man the same treatment as the horse. A red welt appeared along the side of his face. He staggered, falling on the wire before rolling away, his skin ripped by the evil barbs.

Nevit went to help Vincent to his feet but Tyler Bayfield pulled out his gun. The men were angry at Tyler's actions but for now everyone held back, fearful of the wrath of a man tormented by the ghost of his past, and brandishing a weapon.

Russell called out to Tyler.

'Let's get back to the ranch. We serve no purpose here.'

He wanted to get away before something dreadful happened because he reckoned from the look on the men's faces, they'd wrap Tyler in what was left of the barbed wire and skew him into the ground with the wooden posts.

'You have got to kill that renegade Mitch Bayfield,' Tyler said. Russell stared at his brother as they made their way to the 3 Bay Ranch. 'You can do it,' Tyler persisted. 'There's the sheltered pass, not too far from the Pecos River, Dead Man's Gulch, he must use that to cross and get on to our land. It's the quickest route.'

Tyler didn't mention the fact that he'd tried and failed in that very spot. Russell shook his head. He didn't want to be part of this, and told Tyler exactly that. Tyler's face, only inches away, twisted into an evil mask.

'You are part of it.' Tyler laughed with a low guttural sound. 'You were part of it the day you turned back and left him.' Russell cringed but the protests had died on his lips. 'Now you've got to do the job those damn Comanche should've done,' Tyler said.

Kit Bayfield made it plain to everyone he wanted nothing to do with his eldest son when he heard what happened with Vincent. Since Broke appeared, having spent his youth with the Comanche, Kit showed his resentment towards Tyler with everything he said and did.

He bawled him out, in front of all the ranch hands, about his treatment of Joe Vincent. It was as if he was out to take authority from Tyler. He knew he'd accepted their explanation about Mitch probably being dead but Kit knew he should've carried on looking for the kid.

Guilt was the thing that knocked about in his head. Lately it made him so crusty, the cowhands said if he met a rattlesnake he'd let it have the first bite and still come out best. And as Russell sobered, Kit again resorted to drink. The nightmares that tortured his son had now transferred to him, but trouble was, they kept him company during his waking hours as well.

The morning after the argument with Tyler about his use of the whip on a trusty cowhand, Kit Bayfield sobered enough to make a decision. He put his head under the water pump to freshen up and wash the stink of whiskey away. He aimed to ride into town and start to put a few things right. He reasoned there wasn't much he could do to wipe away the years, but if he could make some amends then he'd do it. He rode back a much happier looking man.

It didn't last too long, leastways not after being greeted by the angry faces of Tyler and Russell. He returned to the solace of the bottle, but he felt — tonight at least — he'd have a good night's sleep.

16

Every night of the week, Broke played a game of cat and mouse.

As soon as the 3 Bay Ranch's cowhands replaced the barbed wire he'd cut away, he would return to destroy their handiwork. They never saw or heard him, even though the men sat ready with guns and rifles waiting for him to strike. In the end, unnerved by the silence and the swiftness of his actions, the cowhands stayed by their fires, afraid to venture into the darkness.

Broke was particularly careful as he rode his horse along the narrow path of Dead Man's Gulch. He had good cause to be wary. He'd only just arrived in Pecos County when he'd been used as target practice. The gulch, with its spindly cottonwoods, interspersed with the odd salt cedar tree along the route of a narrow river, and the Ponderosa Pines that grew up the steep sides, was an assassin's dream.

Tonight, as always, he travelled alone. He liked it that way. Gil Tander had volunteered to accompany him on his forays but Tander moved with the grace of a herd of buffalos and Broke refused his aid. His sojourn with the Comanche had taught him how to creep up on an enemy without giving any sign of your presence. It had been so easy with the 3 Bay Ranch cowhands that he had been tempted to help himself to coffee from the pot over the camp-fire.

It was quiet tonight but appearances were deceptive and Broke was aware of everything around him. In the moon-light, he noted every blade of grass, every leaf and pine needle of the trees, as if it were day. He could see the raccoons and squirrels' paths along the ground and where the vultures had disturbed the branches of the high pine trees. He saw the eyes of the owls, a fox hiding behind some high grass, he observed a tarantula scuttling away trying to find somewhere to hide and he heard the flutter of insects' wings as his horse's feet disturbed the undergrowth.

Then an intrusive smell, something out of place with nature, a few yards ahead of him, warned him of something not quite right. He didn't slow his pace, he gave no indication of his suspicions and only the dark pupils of his eyes, dilating a fraction, might have warned whoever was waiting up ahead that Broke knew of their presence.

Tyler convinced Russell he could kill Broke.

'Like shooting tin cans off a fence,' Tyler said.

'OK, Bro',' Russell said. 'You can trust me.'

It was fortunate Russell couldn't see the expression on his brother's face as he rode out with two trusted ranch hands, Hash Morgan and Frank Soar. Both had been with the 3 Bay Ranch for years, moving their allegiance from Kit, to Tyler, with ease. They took their orders from the top dog.

It looked to them as if Tyler had doubts about whether Russell could even cut a lame cow from a shade tree. They heard him promise Russell all the liquor he could drink when he came back with news of their half-brother's death and laughed. Wouldn't cost Tyler too much in booze, especially as his boss had said, related to Frank Soar by Hash Morgan, that with all the bullets flying around the gulch, it wouldn't surprise him if only the two of them came back from Dead Man's Gulch. Tyler had made it plain enough with very few words they were there to kill both brothers tonight. With two kin dead, Tyler Bayfield would inherit the ranch outright.

Russell, as he waited, regretted that he was sober. Life looked better through a haze of liquor. He burped loudly to try to savour the flavour of stale whiskey, which was better than nothing, and licked his lips. He glanced towards the horses they'd left further down the narrow path and now waited hidden above where Broke would pass through the gulch. He wished it would soon be over. As it was, he dug his heels into the slope, leaned against a Ponderosa Pine, and waited for the target to appear.

A soft noise further along Dead Man's Gulch, caused by the movement of Russell digging his heels into the soil, alerted Broke to where the gunman was situated. And from the hiss of voices he also knew that there was more than one man waiting for him. He pressed his thighs into his horse's sides, a signal to it to slow down. He'd taken off the conventional saddle for his nightly forays, changed boots for moccasins, falling back to the Comanche ways to move across an enemy's land. As far as he was concerned, everyone in the Bayfield camp was an enemy.

Broke then threw a stone to land further along the trail, rolled off his horse into the cover of the shrubs and trees, and sent it at a gallop down the path. The ruse worked. He heard shots and what he'd guessed to be Russell's voice. It didn't take much to guess it was Russell, who hadn't been first in the queue for brains, with all that shouting and noise enough to wake a hibernating bear. He came crashing through the trees to find Broke's 'body'.

Broke intended to kill the other men with Russell. Then he wanted to watch his half-brother Russell squirm before dispatching him.

A horse pounded past the three men, Russell, Morgan and Soar. The sound of their guns firing rang through Dead Man's Gulch.

'I told you it'd be easy to kill him,' Russell hollered.

Morgan and Soar looked at one another uneasily. They'd heard that the Bayfield's young half-brother had survived over ten years with the Comanche. He'd returned, not as a timid broken slave, but as a strong young man. And everyone knew he was bent on revenge. So how could it be so easy for Russell, who'd miss the ground if he threw his hat, to shoot him off his horse?

'I'll show that brother of mine how good I am,' he shouted.

The sound of his voice spread right through the gulch and across towards the Lazy Z Ranch.

'Looks as if you've got him right enough,' Morgan agreed. 'We'd best go find him.'

Russell scrambled down towards where he thought the body would be. Morgan held Soar back.

'We'll deal with Russell when we're sure we've only got one brother left to deal with,' Morgan said.

'I'm gonna scalp him,' Russell shouted. Killing seemed to have brought the unsavoury side of his personality to the fore. 'I'm gonna make sure he don't haunt my dreams no more.'

Russell looked around. In his rush he'd left the others behind. Now he was alone. He called out to Morgan and Soar, his voice barely rose above a whisper, although in his ears it sounded far too loud. It began to dawn on him something was wrong. He couldn't see a body. And yet, three against one, his half-brother shouldn't have survived those odds. The hairs at the back of Russell's neck stood on end and something inside him told him that if he hadn't killed his half-brother then he'd become the hunted one.

The two men, Morgan and Soar, waited above. They were happy to let Russell Bayfield go on ahead of them. They'd had more experience of life and knew it didn't always play out as expected. They'd have waited on a while before rushing in. But you couldn't tell a Bayfield what to do, not even a whiskey-soaked lout like Russell.

Morgan didn't want to kill Russell, but Tyler Bayfield owned half the town of Hell and your credit would plummet if you upset one of them. It was as good as being thrown out of town because the other places would be frightened to serve you for fear they'd get into trouble.

When Russell kept shouting that he couldn't find the body, Morgan and Soar relented and went to help. If it had been anyone else they'd have ignored the man, but how to explain the situation to Tyler Bayfield? Well, neither was brave, nor foolhardy enough to do that. Morgan and Soar knew they had a job to do before they could return to the 3 Bay Ranch.

Broke saw the top of Russell's head come into view. He hadn't changed much in the past ten years, Broke thought. As a boy, his lower lip hung down like a blacksmith's apron, and as a man he hadn't turned out too pretty. He still looked like the hindquarters of bad luck. Broke allowed him to rush past and watched for a moment as he thundered through, hollering fit to bust, and then turned his attention to his two cronies.

The men followed slowly after Russell. Broke didn't hesitate. He threw his knife and it landed in the first man's throat. He didn't have time to cry out and to the man walking after him, it was as if he'd stepped into a hole and disappeared.

'Hash! Where are you? You all right?' Soar said.

He scanned the area and couldn't see a thing apart from occasionally glimpsing the bobbing head of Russell as he continued down the slope towards the river. He cupped his mouth with his hands and shouted.

'Russell, you see anything down there?'

Russell heard nothing. A second later he did hear a screech, like a scream cut off. He looked up at the sky for signs of a bird.

'Hash, Frank, you come down here,' he said. 'Don't play games with me.'

In the light of the moon, which the drifting clouds occasionally allowed Broke to see clearly, he noted the mixed emotions cross Russell Bayfield's face. Each one pulled it out of shape as if he'd experienced a spasm of pain. Broke, content to let this continue, lay watching from his hiding place and waited for Russell's next move. Broke could see the man he no longer called brother was deciding whether to stay or run, and hated the weak character, unable to make up his mind.

Then Broke made up his mind for him. He stood up and aimed his gun. Russell saw Broke. A wet patch appeared at the crotch, and ran down the legs of Russell's breeches.

'Time to pay your debts,' Broke said.

The smell of smoke filtered across the gulch from the direction of Lazy Z Ranch. They looked at one another, then a change occurred in Russell's demenour.

'Ha!' His laugh bordered on the edge of hysteria. 'Looks like Tyler got his revenge. You thought you were clever, tormenting us, but my brother said we'd beat you.'

Broke made a quick decision. He didn't have time to deal with Russell. There were a lot of people at the Lazy Z Ranch. He needed to be there to help. But he wasn't going to let Russell get too far away. He took his gun and got ready to aim.

'You ain't gonna kill me in cold blood?' Russell whined.

'And I suppose you were going to give me a chance to defend myself?' Broke asked. Russell shivered with fear. 'No. I'll give you a fair chance to draw, which is more than you gave me. But not now, however I'll make sure you can't run away too far.'

Broke's shot shattered Russell's knee.

'I'll see you later,' Broke said.

He called his horse to his side but got no response other than a soft pitiful whinny. He walked up the hillside and saw the horse lying on the ground. It had been caught in the crossfire of the men's wild bullets. His beautiful Appaloosa horse lay injured. He stroked its head and quietly took out his gun. The horse blew through its nostrils and nuzzled his hand as if to say goodbye.

17

Long before Broke made his way along Dead Man's Gulch, Tyler had assembled thirty of his own men and taken another route to the Lazy Z Ranch. He'd suffered three weeks of Broke's antics. He'd lost fences and cattle — and things cost money. It didn't matter that the salesman told him barbed wire was cheap; it started to get expensive when he had to purchase so much of the stuff.

He knew his half-brother, Mitch, was behind it all.

Tyler and Page had been bickering for the past five years and the old fool had always called on Marshal Jones to help out, but nothing had been done. Page hadn't worked out that the marshal wouldn't do anything because he'd paid him not to. The marshal only wanted to make sure he lived long enough to enjoy his pension.

His other reason for going to the ranch was to capture a prize he'd been after for a couple of years, but one that Page refused to hand over. Lizbeth, his daughter, had grown into a beautiful young woman and, if he married her, Tyler would inherit the Lazy Z Ranch.

A cruel scowl crossed his features. He'd done the proper thing and asked Page if he could court his daughter. He didn't care for her as such but she'd do. He wanted the land she'd bring with her when the old man died. He lied so well about his good intentions that the man was a fool not to believe him. Page hadn't been happy about the proposal but he'd responded as he should and put the question to Lizbeth. Graceful and ladylike in her refusal, Tyler Bayfield still imagined she'd laughed at him when she closed the door. He wasn't going to take a second rebuff. He wasn't going to ask her. He'd take her to the 3 Bay Ranch and force her to live with him as a wife. He reasoned she'd have to marry him then.

Swiftly he turned his mind to the present situation. They were in sight of the Lazy Z Ranch.

'We ride in hard and show them we've had enough. Got your guns ready? Anyone who fights back, looks as if they might resist, shoot them,' he said. He looked towards Joe Vincent. 'You got the torches?'

The sound of flint on metal was the answer and a piece of wood, wrapped with rags doused in oil, was alight. Soon half a dozen were ablaze.

All Gil Tander heard at first was the pounding of horses' hoofs over the hard ground. Before he had time to react they were overrun with gunmen and the shooting started. He'd stationed men on watch but perhaps they'd got lazy because they figured all the action was over at the 3 Bay Ranch.

In seconds, he'd grabbed a Winchester rifle and dashed from the bunkhouse. It was mayhem outside. Immediately Tander identified Tyler Bayfield. Whatever Broke was up to tonight, it hadn't included keeping the Bayfields away from the ranch, he thought. He saw Tyler heading towards the ranch house and followed him.

Tander shut his eyes then opened them again, shaking his head as if to clear an apparition, but it was no figment of his imagination. The sky, much brighter than it ought to be, was lit by a burning house. Several out-buildings were ablaze. The madmen were burning the whole of the Lazy Z Ranch.

Then he saw a scuffle between his boss and Tyler Bayfield. He shot at Tyler but missed. Then a searing pain in his shoulder told him he'd been hit. The blood from his wound made him weak. Regardless of the pain, he kept on his feet and carried on shooting at any man who didn't work for Crosland Page. Several men fell as the bullets hit a target. Tyler dragged Lizbeth from the ranch and towards a waiting horse and Tander had no chance to help her.

Broke left Russell Bayfield to deal

with his shattered kneecap. The man was hollering like a banshee. If Broke felt anything, it was repugnance. He'd learned to control his emotions. No Comanche brave would display, on the face or in behaviour, any emotions or suffering they experienced. He'd watched men being tortured. Many won respect by accepting punishment, even winning their freedom; others had suffered more as they screamed like children. He didn't think Russell would have been reprieved.

He took a horse from one of the three left in the gulch and rode, as fast as he could, across the plains. He already missed his fine steed. As he neared the Lazy Z Ranch, the smoke increased and he could see plumes of flames. It lit up the night sky. He reached the ranch with a heavy heart.

'Gil's down, shot real bad I think,' a cowhand called out. 'Don't know about Mr Page.'

The brief conversation was halted as a bucket got thrust into the man's hand. The Bayfield gang had left the scene. According to the men they'd rode in, guns firing and torches blazing, and out to do as much damage as possible. Someone had shouted that it was payback time for all the broken fences and stolen land. The torches had been thrown at every building and only a few of the cowhands had time to shoot back, once the fires had started, as they'd tried to save as much of the Lazy Z as they could.

The ranch was black and half burnt to the ground and Broke found it difficult to suppress his feelings of dismay as he asked about Crosland Page and Lizbeth.

'I seen Lizbeth going off with Tyler Bayfield. But he weren't none too happy about it 'cause it looked liked he'd picked up a wild cat.'

Broke relaxed slightly on hearing that. He knew Lizbeth was tough. It was said that those afraid of hard work, coyotes, guns and Indians had better not try to make a home in the West. He was concerned about the old man.

He needn't have worried.

Crosland Page's voice shouted over to Broke, 'You gonna sit on that horse all night?'

'No longer than it takes to ride towards the 3 Bay Ranch,' Broke answered. 'You'd better send someone to town for a doctor, I think Tander, amongst others, has got hit by the 3 Bay gang bullets.'

Page noted that Broke had called his family a 'gang' but he didn't comment.

'Watch out for Lizbeth,' he said.

Broke didn't answer. He'd already headed off and, within minutes, showed up as nothing more than a pair of horse's hoofs in the distance.

He knew he might meet up with Russell limping back, as he rode along Dead Man's Gulch, but he wasn't concerned about the possibility. The guns Russell would pick up were minus the ammo. Broke had slung the slugs across the other side of the gulch and it would take Russell a month, or longer, to team the two things up again.

Aiming to stop for nothing or no one, Broke was determined to travel faster than a ball from an army cannon. The poor horse tried to speed up to his expectations and struggled bravely. Tyler would be under the impression that Broke was dead because he'd sent two extra gunslingers to shoot him in case his brother missed. Broke was sure they wouldn't be telling him otherwise. The blowflies would be feasting on the men, together with the buzzards, as soon as the sun came up.

It wasn't far from that time now, he noted. The fingers of the sun's rays showed above the horizon as he slowed the horse. He'd reached halfway into the Bayfield territory — though not strictly theirs because they'd filched land from neighbours like Crosland Page, or they'd plain run people off their land and taken over what had been left. All in all, they'd acquired a pretty good spread.

They seemed above the law. Marshal Jones didn't pursue any wrongdoers 'if it happened outside of town'.

They owned stores in town and they held people in hock. It dampened opposition if a man got threatened with foreclosure — and foreclose they would if a farmer or rancher gave a Bayfield brother trouble and stepped out of line.

18

'You little . . . '

Tyler Bayfield didn't manage to finish his words. He sucked at the wound Lizbeth had given him.

'She's got a fine set of teeth.'

The man who thought it was funny ate his words. Tyler landed his fist straight on his mouth. The dazed man sat spitting blood. Others, with more experience of Tyler's temper, shook their heads at the man's foolish quip. They knew it was better to keep your mouth shut.

Tyler left her alone now, confident she couldn't escape, but wary of her after the spat they'd had. He scowled and threatened to get even when this was all over. Now he got on with the task of stationing his men around the place knowing that Crosland Page would be on his trail as soon as he could. He knew he should've killed the rancher but fore-man Tander had come close to wounding him. He'd had to make a run for it.

Lizbeth saw the man fall to the ground and backed away as far as she could from Tyler. He'd bound her wrists together and she used her only sharp weapon, her teeth. Now she hoped he wouldn't think to gag her or worse.

It had been a complete surprise, the attack on the ranch, and yet they ought to have been expecting it. It made her wonder whether her pa might not be getting old, but she shook the thought away as if it was the worse thing that could've crept into her mind. She had to cling on to the hope that he'd be organizing his men to come and rescue her. However, she knew his first priority would be to save the cattle and the ranch.

The men at the Lazy Z were busy trying to save the buildings and live-stock, and Broke was on his way to get Lizbeth from Tyler's clutches. He'd dis-missed the idea of asking for Marshal

Jones's help. He wasn't sure whether the marshal would lock him up if he stepped across the town's boundary again.

Broke's mind was also on facing Tyler with what he'd done years ago. He'd always vowed to kill him. That had kept him going when the Comanche had first captured him. Not that he'd wasted all his time hating. His adopted mother, Beautiful, had been kind and his adopted father, Fighting Bear, was one of the wisest men he'd ever known. In many ways he'd enjoyed his time with the Indian people.

It was the fact that he'd been denied his rightful place in his own family that angered him. He was an outcast. He didn't fit in any camp. White men were uneasy around him, not quite treating him as one of theirs, and he'd left the Indian encampment when Beautiful had died following a short illness. He owed his acceptance to her and even though his many acts of bravery had earned him a place in the tribe, he felt unsettled, and left to go back to his old life. The young woman, Little Bluestem, came unbidden into his head. She, like him, had been kidnapped from her family and because of that connection he'd helped her through the first few weeks with the Comanche and they'd become good friends.

Up ahead he saw the 3 Bay Ranch. Broke knew that if he got too close, the Bayfield men would soon spot him. He left the now tired horse, with its bridle looped over a stone buried into the ground, grazing on prairie grass, and made his way on foot. His skills came into play, as he covered the ground, from the horse to the ranch, quicker than syrup flowing from a hot pan.

His knife and his Colt Frontier were in his belt and he carried his trusty Henry rifle. He slung ammunition across his chest in a couple of holsters. He had no intention of losing this battle. He knew he could move fast enough to make them think they were facing more than one man.

Tyler had posted look-outs but had

only put a couple of men on the roof. Broke took advantage of the fact that they couldn't look everywhere and moved speedily across the ground.

Lenny saw and heard nothing. He didn't turn when Broke came up behind him. Then an arm came round his throat. Lenny's natural instinct to cry out was cut short as a blade sliced through his wind-pipe. He only sensed warmth as the hot blood gushed out and down and over his neck and chest.

Broke saw the man's eyes glaze over and let his body fall slowly and silently to the ground. Then he moved on towards the next one.

Inside the ranch house, Tyler became uneasy. He'd expected Page to do something. And yet two hours had passed and nothing had happened. He looked out the window.

'Go and check with Lenny and Mo. Make sure they're on the job and not taking a smoke.'

Vincent and Nevit glanced at each other. They hoped that was the reason and it made them all feel a whole lot better hearing it. The alternative was too awful to contemplate.

'OK, boss,' Vincent said.

He took care not to disagree with whatever Tyler said. He still bore a scar where Bayfield had lost his temper and brandished his whip.

Outside, from his hiding place, Broke saw the door opening a crack, and a cowhand slip out. He didn't know how many were in the ranch house but he'd find out. He'd seen several men walking around, however the blade of his knife had already thinned their numbers. He hadn't taken out the two on the roof yet. He was wary of shooting until he had to.

On the ground lay a thin hand-rolled cheroot with a wisp of smoke spiralling upwards. Vincent smiled. 'Looks like Tyler was right,' he said. Then he followed a trail that led him to Lenny's body.

Vincent pulled out his gun. He shouted names of other men but, hearing only a few replies, he started to run back towards the ranch house. Shots peppered the air around him and he dived to the floor. Tyler refused to open the door.

'Stay outside and find out how many are out there,' Tyler said.

He had no sympathy for others. He wouldn't open the door and endanger himself. Inside the ranch house he looked at the girl and briefly saw a look of disgust on her face. Then she'd lowered her eyelids and judiciously concealed her feelings from him. Anyone who knew Tyler wouldn't have thought anything of it, but he'd only come to Lizbeth's notice as she got older, and he'd seen her as a potential marriage partner. He'd acted as sweet as honey to try and win her hand, but as he'd tell his drinking pals when on a bender, he'd have married her, even if she'd been ugly as a mud fence.

If a girl had a parcel of land like the Lazy Z for a dowry it would make even a burnt boot appear beguiling.

19

A bullet whizzed into Broke.

He poked his fingers through the hole in his hat, shaking his head at the notion that had the shot been a little more to the left, not only his bowler would been vented by bullet holes, but his head. Luckily it was a wild shot, rather than a bullet from a well-aimed gun.

It came from Joe Vincent's gun. The old-timer had spun across the porch and to the side of the building. Broke cursed that he hadn't managed to hit him but unfortunately the feller jumped around like a monkey. He'd taken the two off the roof and watched as they hit the ground with shattering thuds.

Broke's eyes focused on the dark points of the landscape — to the sides of the ranch and inside the barn and outbuildings — from shuttered windows. Each time he saw the flash of gunpowder as a gun fired, he took aim and shot back. He moved around, never staying in the same place, to avoid the bullets fired at him. Now he crept towards the barn on the far side of the building, well away from the ranch house. He'd seen several guns fired from there.

He didn't think anyone was in the bunkhouse but he slipped inside before going any further. It was a singular building that looked vulnerable and exposed. It was clear of men and gave the impression of something left in a hurry. The plates of half eaten victuals, up-ended chairs and even a pair of boots, made it seem as if the whole caboodle had run away. They had probably rushed out to fight and were now holed up in the barn.

Like a fox after a hen-house, he crept along using any ranch debris on the ground to cover his journey to the barn. His muscular body, fine-tuned as an athlete, enabled him to scale up the barn wall, using the natural knots in the wood and the dovetail joints, where the building was fixed together to get to the high opening that led to a loft overlooking the barn floor.

Broke observed five men, all of whom he thought were plumb weak north of their ears. They crowded round the doorway as if waiting for their assailants to attack. It hadn't occurred to them that no one was likely to run straight towards them. The fact that his opponents probably couldn't track a bed wagon through a bog hole was an advantage to Broke. He'd have to win the fight quickly because once it started, likely as not, it would alert those in the ranch house and all hell would break out.

He raised his Henry rifle and aimed. He liked to give a man a chance but it wasn't the time to be a gentleman. Three were down before the other two had time to turn and react. And when they did, it was too late.

Broke ran down the ladder, and out the barn and made his way towards the ranch house. The lack of reaction to

176

the gunfire surprised him. Maybe Tyler had already fled the place and left him shooting at ghosts. He paused and took a few seconds to regain his breath and take some thinking time. A few seconds was too long. He felt a gun prod uncomfortably into his back.

'Did you think you were so smart,' Tyler Bayfield whispered, 'that you thought you could finish us off single-handed?'

Broke didn't reply. The words soaked into his ears, louder than if they'd been shouted. It had been his plan and it hadn't gone right. It had been a simple rather than smart plan. He wanted to finish the job of killing his two brothers and rescuing Page's daughter, Lizbeth. At the moment he knew he was beaten, so he dropped the rifle and held up his hands. Tyler took his Colt Frontier and tucked it into his own belt. He forced Broke to move forwards by jabbing the gun into him and it seemed to him that he'd be meeting everyone shortly. It wasn't in the circumstances he'd foreseen. He hadn't intended to become the captive instead of the captor.

'Broke!'

Lizbeth tried to run towards him but Russell pulled her back. The action caused him great pain because his knee, crudely bound with bloody rags, couldn't support the shattered bones. Broke saw from the evil grimace he got, his half-brother would like to see him suffer as much as he suffered now. In case he hadn't got the message, Russell lifted his gun and smashed the butt against the side of Broke's head. With a grimace of agony, Broke fell to the floor. Russell tried to kick him in the side with his good leg, but fell as the other leg gave way unable to take the weight and the pain. Tyler grabbed his brother before he hit the floor.

'Are you stupid'?' he asked. 'Stop playing around. I brought him in here so you could see me kill him. It'll put an end to your nightmares, brother. This way you'll know he's dead and he won't come back anymore.' He turned towards his pa who sat in the corner of the room. Kit Bayfield seemed dazed by everything. 'And you, old man, keep the gun squarely on her. If she moves I want you to pull that trigger.'

Then Tyler moved closer to Lizbeth. He skilfully avoided being too near, in case she took a fancy to bite him again. However it was she who recoiled as his fetid breath washed over her. He laughed.

'Get used to it. I've had enough of paying for female company from Miss Kitty's lodging-house.' He took delight in her distress. 'No use looking for any help because we've killed everyone from the Lazy Z, including your father.'

Lizbeth's face contorted with grief. After her initial cheer at seeing Broke, she sat quietly in a chair, all fight drained from her.

Broke had feigned being knocked out. When Russell hit him, he'd moved his head slightly and the wound was superficial. However it gave him time to think out his next move. He still had his knife. Tyler, so pleased he'd snuck up on his half-brother, hadn't checked him for more weapons than he'd offered up. Broke's heart was pained by the lies Tyler had told Lizbeth to subdue and hurt her but it wasn't the time to say anything. He saw his pa sitting next to Lizbeth — he looked as much a prisoner as she was. Broke had no feelings towards the man. After all, it was his sons who wanted to kill him and he wasn't doing a thing to stop them.

And yet perhaps Tyler did think his men had killed Page and all the hands at the Lazy Z Ranch. Broke knew that as soon as the fire was out, Page would be riding to 3 Bay Ranch and hollering for blood. Despite his resolution never to show emotion, his lips pulled into a thin smile. It went unnoticed by everyone except Lizbeth and he figured the slight movement would give her a glimmer of hope that her predicament wasn't hopeless. One thing he was sure about was that it was unlikely Tyler would kill him while he lay on the floor.

Tyler, always bordering on theatrical as a youth, would make a spectacle of it.

'Get me some water,' Tyler said. Russell handed him a saucepan of cold liquid. 'Not last night's stew, idiot,' Tyler berated him. 'No, on second thoughts, it'll do.'

He threw the concoction over Broke. If Broke had intentions of playing dumb, the taste of rabbit stew changed that. He spat the stuff from his mouth as he shook his head. Tyler hauled Broke from the floor and stood him against the wall.

'Not so high and mighty now eh?' Tyler said.

'Don't taste too good,' Broke said. 'Pity you won't be able to enjoy something better than that again.'

Tyler frowned.

'Why's that?' he asked.

'Because you won't be around to eat it,' Broke replied.

In response, Tyler hit Broke with his fist. Broke staggered from the blow and fell against his half-brother, who hit him again. He went spinning across the room with the force of the blow.

'Seems to me, little brother, you ain't gonna be doing too much eating yourself,' he said.

Lizbeth's face filled with despair. Tears were in her eyes as she wondered how much of a beating Broke would be able to take. Russell answered the unspoken question for her.

'We gonna beat him to a pulp, eh, Tyler?'

Tyler shot a disdainful look in Russell's direction. They both knew that if Russell had done his job properly, this question wouldn't have needed asking. Russell looked away, unable to bear the grimace on his brother's face. This was the opportunity Broke had waited for. No one noticed that when Tyler hit him, he'd fallen and staggered around to cover up the fact he'd used his knife to cut himself free. He lunged forward. Tyler, now in Broke's steelly grip, lost his balance.

'Shoot him!' Tyler cried.

Russell made a pathetic attempt to shoot Broke. The bullets thudded into the floor as Lizbeth jumped up and jolted his arm with her shoulder as he fired the gun. Roughly he pushed her back on to the chair.

'Don't you try anything else,' he warned.

His gun waved menacingly at her. He tried to fire again but it was difficult to avoid hitting Tyler as the pair rolled across the floor, so he lowered his gun. Then there was a crash and a smashing sound as the door came off its hinges. Broke and Tyler were now outside through the opening where the door had been. Entwined as if they were one, Russell watched to see which brother would be the victor. He'd always assumed that Tyler could do anything and yet here he was, literally brought to his knees by the half-brother he swore wouldn't ever trouble them again.

Tyler got the first victory. He was on top of Broke, his hands round his neck. Then Broke brought his legs up together and the force of the kick threw Tyler off. Tyler got to his feet quickly for a large man. He was fast on the draw and pulled out his iron to aim a Colt .45 at Broke. His thumb pulled back the trigger but Broke had a knife in his hand and threw it. Tyler's reaction saved him from being gutted. He veered to the left to avoid the knife, but the gun was knocked from his hand.

Broke took a knife from his boot and thrust the knife at Tyler. It found a target and tore into flesh. Tyler was wounded and blood poured down his arm.

'You had that all the time?'

Amazement showed on Tyler's face at Broke's arsenal of weapons. He also looked dizzy from the loss of blood and stumbled. Broke watched and allowed him to regain his footing.

'I had my own knife but when I fell on to you, I took your knife as well.'

Tyler's hand automatically went to his belt. His face supplied the words.

He looked both incredulous and angry that he'd been so easily fooled. Broke retrieved the knife and offered it to Tyler.

'We're equal now, we can fight until one of us dies.'

'You're wrong if you think we're equal. We've never been that. You're an interloper who never belonged in this family. The day those Comanche took you should've been the last we saw of you,' Tyler said. 'We saw the Injuns had got you. Me and Russell decided it was the best thing that could've happened and we turned round and came home.'

Broke allowed one eyebrow to rise. The movement said more than a whole conversation. Tyler didn't seem to realize the gravity of his words.

'Russell or Pa will kill Lizbeth if I tell them. They will too,' Tyler ranted.

Broke knew a man with too much anger would be easily beaten. Anger equals loss of concentration and control. It means a slip that can lose a battle or a life. Broke didn't want it to be too quick. He wanted Tyler to feel pain.

His two brothers owed him twelve years of his life.

20

Swiftly Broke's hand moved and the sun caught the flash of the knife. Tyler saw nothing. He felt pain and blood running down the side of his face. His hand went to his ear and his face mirrored everyone's disbelief at what had happened to him.

'My ear,' he cried.

'That's for the calls for help that you refused to hear,' Broke said. 'Perhaps your hearing will be sharper now.'

'Russell, Russell,' Tyler called. 'Shoot him why don't you?'

Russell stood in the space of the doorway. He shook from head to foot. He could see Tyler was going to lose.

Tyler glared at Russell and then at Broke.

'You damned Comanche,' he said.

'I stopped calling for help,' Broke continued. It was as if Tyler hadn't asked Russell to shoot. 'I learned that the Comanche don't like weakness. So I held my tongue. Now you'll hold yours.'

Tyler didn't understand. Broke moved swiftly. His arm wrapped round Tyler's neck forcing him to gag. Lizbeth screamed and ran towards the men. Kit Bayfield had untied her hands and they'd followed Broke, Tyler and Russell outside. The spell that kept her feet stuck to the floor after Broke had cut Tyler's ear dissolved and she found it possible to move again. Broke held Tyler in a stranglehold and had his knife ready to cut out his tongue.

'Broke!' Lizbeth cried.

He pressed the blade on Tyler's tongue and a thin red line appeared. Lizbeth grabbed hold of Broke's arm and shook him.

'Don't! You'll be as bad as them, the Comanche and your half-brothers, if you do this. And what next? Will you cut out his eyes because he didn't look far enough for you? If you're the man you say you are, at least let him have the chance to draw his gun. Have a shoot out. Make it clean.'

The glaze that had dropped over Broke's eyes receded. He blinked, looked at Tyler and let him fall to the ground. Kit Bayfield walked over to his son and Broke waited for him to say something.

'I'm sorry, Mitch,' he said. 'Shoot it out with me. I'm the one who should pay. When these boys returned, I should've carried on searching 'til I found you.'

Broke shook his head. His usually passive features revealed a flash of sorrow then it was gone.

'I've made the ranch over to you, Mitch,' Kit said. 'I disowned these sons as soon as you turned up and I knew they'd left you out there.'

Russell stopped shaking and shouted at his Pa, 'You did what? You gave everything to him? Tyler and me ain't gonna get anything? Why, I'm gonna kill you for that.'

He aimed his gun at him but never got chance to pull the trigger. Kit

Bayfield fired first. Russell Bayfield uttered no more threats. As Tyler got up, he went for his Peacemaker.

'You're a traitor, Pa,' he said. 'No way is that half-brother, or should I say half-breed, gonna take what's mine. I'm gonna kill him and he'll never get my land.'

He wasn't quick enough to kill Broke. The knife that was going to cut out his tongue cut the gun right out of his hand and pinned his sleeve of his coat to the ground.

'Do what Lizbeth said. Fight this out on equal terms,' Kit Bayfield said.

As the blood poured from his ear, Tyler spat on the ground.

'He had to handicap me before he thought he had a chance,' he sneered.

'Let me patch you up first,' Lizbeth offered.

'I don't need a woman to help me out. I'll fight my own battles.'

'Do as she says,' Kit Bayfield ordered.

Reluctantly he let the girl bind a bandage round his head to stop the bleeding from his ear and tended the arm wound from the earlier skirmish. But he wouldn't relent about fighting it out with his 'half-breed half-brother', as he now called him. This time there was to be no gun, no knives, only fists. Kit insisted on that. No matter what the brothers had done, he didn't want to see another one killed.

'Now knock the tar out of each other if you have to,' he said.

The two men circled each other. They both kept their distance as they summed each other up. Stripped to the waist, a betting man would've have placed his money on Broke rather than Tyler. It was plain to everyone that Tyler was unfit. The man was older and had spent too long propping up bars in saloons. Years of indulgence had left him unable to defend himself as well as Broke, who'd lived a completely different life. His Comanche family raised him to be strong in body and mind and the nomadic lifestyle had given him stamina.

Broke looked at Tyler. Blood seeped through the bandage on his ear and made a thick red patch on the left side of Tyler's head. His face scrunched with pain but Tyler had his left arm out, fist clenched, ready to place a jabbing cut if he found the opportunity.

On the surface it was uneven but hate was in Tyler's eyes.

There was no love lost between them.

Broke held his hands up ready to protect his mouth and chin from Tyler's fists. His stance mirrored his half-brother's, except his body was held lower to minimize the chance of Tyler landing a blow, and his feet were placed wide to give balance, as they moved round each other ready to throw the first punch.

Broke got in the first jab. Tyler, unbalanced and slow, caught it on the chin and reeled backwards. His brother gave him a chance to recover but the moment was brief and as Tyler straightened his body to standing, his fist hit Broke's unguarded body in the gut. His arms extended to their full length and he punished Broke's body. He fell and Tyler followed through with kicks. Broke rolled away and got to his feet. Now it was his turn. He hit Tyler in the chest. Tyler's lungs gasped for air. Broke waited again. Then they circled, watching and waiting, ready to grab the opportunity for an attack. Both looked for the other to drop his guard. That didn't happen.

Broke's hard muscular bronzed body showed little sign of the punches he'd received, yet Tyler was white and pallid, with his skin beginning to turn purple and blue.

Kit and Lizbeth watched and waited on the outcome. Lizbeth looked troubled; she had seen too much anger and bloodshed over the past few hours. The lines in Kit's face deepened. The body of one son lay on the ground, rolled against the porch, waiting to be buried. A few fat flies buzzed around the wound.

Tyler staggered like a drunk. His face had received a beating and his right eye had closed into little more than a slit. It puffed up and oozed red fluid. Broke didn't think he could see through the eye at all. Tyler came towards him again, lunging and stepping up close to get an uppercut to Broke's body. Broke looked as if he admired Tyler's efforts but that's all they were — efforts to try and bring him down — and a swift retaliation had Tyler on the ground again.

This time Broke didn't wait for him to get up. He pounced and, straddled across the fallen man, he punched him, one fist following the other, mercilessly, in rapid succession.

If anyone had looked into his eyes they'd have been able to see a red mist there. Rage took over and he lost his control as the hatred of years over-whelmed him.

'That's enough, Son.'

Through the haze, the softly spoken words had the desired effect. He got up and walked away from the wreck of a man he'd left lying on the floor.

He stopped and turned towards his father.

'Keep your ranch, Pa,' Broke said. 'Alter the will so it goes to Tyler. He's the eldest. I don't want it.'

Broke looked sick. He looked as if he wanted to leave and never return to this place.

'I've made it over to you,' Kit Bayfield said. 'You might not have plans yet but think it through. Tyler has never had much interest in this place. I'll pay him off. I haven't many years left and I want to know it will be looked after. What you going to do? Let it go to seed? Or worse, let someone else take it?'

Broke picked up his knife, rifle and gun. He shook his head.

'I don't belong here,' he said. 'Best you send for the doc to patch up Tyler.' He looked round at the dead men. 'You'll need the undertaker as well.'

There was silence as Broke and Lizbeth rode through Dead Man's Gulch. Lizbeth, still traumatized by events, seemed to want nothing more than her own company. Broke respected this and didn't intrude by trying to make conversation. It wasn't his way. He was more than happy to keep his own counsel. He fitted in with the western way of doing things. It was a land for new beginning and accepting that men, and women, had past lives they wanted to leave behind.

Crosland Page stood amongst the ruins of his ranch and his daughter slipped from the horse's saddle and ran over to him. Broke dismounted but kept back from the pair. It was a time for family and he didn't belong. He went over to the bunkhouse, which hadn't suffered as badly as the ranch, to find out about Gil Tander and how the other hands had fared in the attack.

'Howdy.'

A familiar voice greeted him as he walked through the door. Tander's yellow-white teeth stood out in a soot-blackened face. The man had one arm in a sling but with his other he searched through a box of tools.

'Glad to see you,' Broke said.

He clasped the man's good shoulder with his hand. It was the closest the two ever came to a friendly embrace. Both stepped back and Tander, overcome with emotion, cleared his throat and explained about the day's events.

'Page was about to round up some men to go after Lizbeth,' he said. 'I told him you'd gone chasing after her and she'd be all right.'

'Thanks for your faith in me,' Broke said. 'What's happening here?'

'Can't do much to help,' Tander said. 'I can just about knock a few nails in planks, so that's what I'm about to do.'

He picked up a hammer from the box and swung it in his good hand. He explained that everyone who could help had started to pull down the ruins, salvage anything useful, and cut down trees to rebuild.

'I see nothing stops the Lazy Z,' Broke said. 'Got a hammer I could use?'

Tander threw his hammer to Broke

and fished in the box for another one for himself.

'That sure is right,' Tander agreed. 'Got to get everything rolling again.'

'Did anyone get badly hurt?' Broke asked. He looked at Tander's shoulder. 'You had a doc look that over?'

'I'll be OK. The cook bandaged us all up. Seems he makes a better doc than he does a cook, or we'd all be dead.' Tander smiled then his face clouded over as he recalled the other men who'd not been so lucky. 'We're going over and make them pay for this,' he said.

'They've already paid their debts,' Broke said. 'Not many 3 Bay men standing. Russell is dead.' He saw the look on Tander's face and added, 'Pa shot him. I fought with Tyler. He's nursing his wounds. Only Pa was standing upright when I left. Joe Vincent, an old hand, is helping him. I know Pa didn't have a hand in any of this carnage.' He looked around at the wreckage the 3 Bay men had left. 'The only crime he's guilty of is raising boys who turned out bad. But then men make their own choices when they're grown. We can't blame our parents, can we?'

Tander nodded in agreement.

Everyone from town came to help. In a few days, Crosland Page and Lizbeth had somewhere decent to live.

Then everyone's thoughts turned to someone else who needed their help.

21

All the townsfolk were lined up ready to
go.

'We left you in the hands of those
Injuns,' Cutler said. 'We won't let it
happen again.'

It seemed to Broke that all their faces
were etched with lines. One for every
day he'd been missing and they'd not
gone to find him.

'We owe you, as much as the
young'un, to go look for him and bring
him back.'

'They'll kill him if you go in as a
lynch mob looking for a fight — not
only the kid's life but your own will be
forfeit,' Broke said.

'Well, if we don't succeed,' Page said,
'he's better off dead.'

The man who'd spent his youth with
the Comanche thought deeply about
this. His life hadn't been bad, just not

right. He was glad to be alive. And he said this much to them.

'You were right, son, when you rode back into town with vengeance in your heart,' Marshal Jones said. 'The town does owe you. I shouldn't have let your half-brothers persuade me otherwise. I, we, let you down.'

The marshal, nearing retirement, looked even older than he had before. The events of the last few days had aged him and, where silver had been mixed with strands of light brown hair, it had now been replaced by a flat metallic grey.

Broke pleaded with them, 'Let me go and talk to the Comanche.'

Crosland Page seemed the most sympathetic towards Broke's idea. He looked towards the others. Angry words were exchanged but he spoke quietly to them and then he turned to Broke.

'You go and speak to the Comanche. But no way are you going alone. We're with you every step of the way. And if we don't succeed then we'll bring in the army.'

It was all Broke could hope for and with a gentle pull on the reins and the slight pressure from his knees, the horse responded and moved forward away from the men. He cantered off towards the Comanche reservation. He believed he had very little chance of success.

The dust churned up by the horses' hoofs signalled their approach long before the thunderous noise they made reached the ears of the Comanche.

As the men got nearer, it was obvious they were outnumbered. They saw the Indian, who Broke informed them was a great warrior named Fighting Bear, with his sons Black Horse and Wolf Slayer. Together, headed a band of a hundred braves.

'You sure this is a good idea?' Jan Coots said.

Some folk were apprehensive about moving forward when they saw the strength of their opposition.

'There's no chance of going back now,' Page said.

He wasn't one for backing off from a

situation but he could understand the nervous tension in the men round him. The Indians were in full war paint, with faces and bodies daubed in all colours. They looked ferocious opponents. He was also aware that if the Indians sensed any fear they'd be after them. The townsfolk would end up with more holes than a miner's sieve, with arrows and bullets peppering their bodies.

'Yes, you're right,' Jan Coots agreed. 'Let's charge right at them Injuns now.'

Broke held up his hand to quell the noisy discussion between the men.

'If we do, we'll kill a few, more than a few maybe, I'll grant you that,' he said. The men were well armed with shotguns and rifles. 'But there will be quite a few families back in town without a man to look out for them.'

He paused. He could see from the men's faces that the enormity of what they were doing was gradually sinking in.

'Let me do what I suggested in the first place,' Broke said.

'I vote we get the army involved. They should've been the first to tackle something like this,' Marshal Jones said.

'It's too late for the army. We're here and they're not,' Page said. Dissenting murmurs greeted these words. 'Let the Bayfield boy go in first to try and parley with them.'

He added this as he could see that many of the 'brave' men of the town were ready to bolt for cover. The trouble was, there wasn't anywhere to go.

Broke zigzagged his horse towards the Comanche warriors. It was a dance that signalled his peaceful intentions. His adopted father Fighting Bear greeted him.

'My son, Broke, why are you with these palefaces who come to make war on us?' he asked.

'The townsfolk have come to ask for the boy, Forest Hutting, to be returned.'

'Come to ask?' Wolf Slayer interrupted. 'These people are here to fight with us.'

'They are ready to fight because

you've attacked their homes. This boy was kidnapped.'

'We attacked because they have broken yet another treaty with the Indian people,' Black Horse added.

The two young Comanche braves, as well as being decorated with war paint, had Quill feathers in their plaited hair. They were eager to fight and earn their place as warriors within the tribe.

'I know this has happened, Black Horse, Wolf Slayer,' Broke said. 'But the treaty was broken by the army and not the ordinary folk here. The army is powerful. If you fight these men today, for every man here, a hundred soldiers will follow.'

'You have gone over to them,' Black Horse said. 'I can no longer call you brother.'

He spat on to the ground and cursed Broke.

'You were with us from the moment we were born,' Wolf Slayer said. 'And yet you chose the way of the palefaces against ours.'

The situation here, Broke knew, could explode like a stick striking a hornet's nest, and with consequences a million times worse.

'I would not have changed the time I spent with you,' Broke said.

In that moment, Broke knew the words he spoke were true. It lifted the bitterness he'd felt towards his family and the people of Hell, and dissolved any resentment towards the Comanche. It didn't make anything right, but Broke accepted that sometimes things happen and you've just got to get on with life. Perhaps it was a genuineness inside him which made the Indians listen to his words.

'Imagine if the palefaces had taken one of the Comanche children and forced him to learn their ways?'

'Never!'

Black Horse's furious reply sounded like a bullet from a gun. His reaction showed he'd never considered the possibility. Fighting Bear now spoke. He'd allowed the three young men to converse without interruption.

'Broke is right. We have to give the boy back to his own family. We are not his people.'

Black Horse lifted his spear and his Winchester rifle.

'I vote that we fight these palefaces. And the army.'

'I order you,' Fighting Bear said. 'My word is final.'

Both his sons looked rebellious. They knew they could force a council of war and override their father if enough young braves wanted to fight. Broke figured it would cause a lot of trouble in the area to have a band of renegade braves looking for a fight.

'Perhaps we could do this with honour on all sides,' he suggested.

The townsfolk watched the Indians and Broke from a distance. They knew the discussion wasn't easy and it seemed, from where they were placed, that the talk hadn't gone their way. Most checked their guns and rifles and hoped they'd made peace with their

Lord, and got ready for the next stage of their journey — the fight for the boy, Forest.

They saw Broke riding back towards them and waited to hear what he had to say.

'They will let the boy return,' Broke said.

'And what price do we have to pay?'

Crosland Page knew the Indians well enough to know that a gift given means a gift is expected in return.

'We let the two young warriors, Black Horse and Wolf Slayer, earn their honour by touching the senior men here.'

'What!'

Broke explained that to touch an enemy was a greater honour than killing that person. The boys were at an age when they could earn their right to hunt and fight, and this would be a way of proving how brave they were. They and a few other young braves would use coup sticks, or their hands to touch them.

'So I've promised them that ten of the bravest, most important people in town, will stand down and allow them to do just that.'

'What guarantee do we have that they'll return the child?' Page asked.

'They've promised,' Broke said.

'You're taking the word of an Injun?'

'I ain't gonna stand and let a dirty Injun touch me!'

Broke glanced at the man.

'You ain't important enough. Stay where you are.'

The men were unhappy and Crosland Page saw the situation becoming heated and nasty. He got down from his horse.

'Am I important enough?' he asked.

Broke nodded. Then Marshal Jones got off his horse and stood beside the rancher. Slowly several others joined them. Broke told the rest to keep back from the men waiting for the Indians.

'And throw your guns to the ground where I can see them,' he said.

'Don't you trust us?'

Broke looked at the one who'd asked the question.

'I don't trust a man who don't help save a young boy.' He looked at the other men. 'And I don't want to risk a hot-head taking it on himself to shoot an Indian.'

'What about your gun?'

'I'll keep it.' He rode along the line of men and checked none was armed. 'This is what I call the deadline,' he said. 'Anyone crosses it — they're dead.'

The men who'd elected to be 'touched' by the young warriors waited. They all kept their weapons. They told Broke they'd shoot if they thought they were in danger from the braves.

He lifted his hand to Fighting Bear to indicate the men were ready. Soon afterwards, a group of young Comanche galloped across the plains. They looked fearsome.

Marshal Jones's finger rested on his trigger. As much as he wanted his pension, if he thought one of the redskins was overstepping the mark, he'd fire and die like a man. It wasn't his plan to be a sitting target. Crosland Page stood shoulder to shoulder with him.

'Easy, Marshal,' he said.

After the first tense few seconds, it was clear that the braves were not going to kill them — but they didn't relax. They kept themselves ready. Soon it was over and the Comanche youngsters rode off.

'Don't want to go through that again,' Marshal Jones grumbled.

'What on earth . . . ?'

The Indians had vanished. The whole line of Comanche had disappeared into thin air.

Marshal Jones threw his hat on the floor in disgust. 'We did that,' he shouted, 'and what for?'

He wasn't the only disgruntled person in the group.

'I told you we should've got the army involved from the start.'

Then it all went quiet.

A pony, so dark its brown coat,

could've been mistaken for black, with a blonde mane and tail, came into view. Its fearless rider came right up to the men. He didn't say anything but stopped long enough for a small figure to dismount. The boy said, 'Aquetan, Black Horse.'

22

Broke decided to go. It was time. There was nothing to keep him here any longer. The boy had been returned home to his mother.

He'd said all he was going to say to his pa and his half-brother, Tyler. He had no intention of staying at 3 Bay Ranch.

It was time to say his goodbyes to the ranch owner, Crosland Page. The man wouldn't let him go that easy. The ranch house had been rebuilt and he asked him in to have a look round the new place.

'Got some coffee on the boil. Come and join me. Tell me your plans. If you've a mind to,' he added.

Broke had no wish to stay and discuss anything, but Crosland had asked him and it seemed rude to decline the invitation. The house was comfortable and although sparsely furnished at the moment, Broke had a notion that Lizbeth would soon be nagging her pa to buy stuff to replace what had been destroyed. He only concerned himself with the cowman's real losses.

'What about your stock? All the horses and cattle?' Broke asked.

'When Tyler Bayfield rode over with all his men, they made such a noise, the cattle stampeded. Got some cowboys out on the prairies, rounding them up,' Page grinned. 'They burnt a few buildings down but fortunately we'll recover. How those brothers of yours managed to run a ranch for as long as they did is a mystery to me.' The smile slipped. 'Sorry. Lizbeth told me Russell was dead.'

'Nothing to be sorry about,' Broke said.

'So what you going to do now?' Crosland Page asked. Broke shook his head, saying he had no particular plans. Then Lizbeth joined them and sat with a mug of coffee.

'Broke's got to sort out where he belongs, Pa,' she said. 'At the moment he's half-Comanche and half-white.'

The two stared at each other.

'Lizbeth, that ain't no way to talk to someone,' Crosland Page scolded his daughter. Broke knew he'd acted like the 'savages' his brothers had taunted him about. It was Lizbeth who'd pulled him from the brink.

'She's right. And that's why I need to get away from here. There's too many bad memories. I lived in Hell as a child, best I don't remain here as a man,' he said.

'The town of Hell — why it's just a quirky name, like yours. You can stay and make it a private paradise. Why, you could stay here and marry my daughter. That way you'd eventually have the biggest spread in the county.'

'Pa! Don't you say things like that,' Lizbeth flushed with embarrassment. She walked away, but not before she added; 'And no girl in her right mind would marry a man named Broke.'

'A man can change anything he wants in this country,' Page said. 'Including a damn fool name like Broke. Ain't that right, son?'

Broke's face softened with a smile.

'I suppose a man could,' he said. 'But I ain't ready to settle yet.'

'What about the land? You and Tyler will inherit it one day. You ain't gonna leave it to rot, 'cause Tyler will never look after it.'

'I've told Pa I don't want it. I don't think I'll ever return to these parts.'

'What about that daughter of mine?' Page asked. 'She'd make you a good wife.'

Broke smiled but shook his head. 'Lizbeth's a fine young woman but I don't think I'll fit into her heart. And I've got someone who already has a place in mine.' In his mind he saw Little Bluestem. 'First though, I need to take a look at the world. A man who feels like that wouldn't be honourable if he made promises he couldn't keep. She's got someone here who'd suit her. Gil Tander. He's ten years older but perhaps that's not a bad thing.'

Crosland Page's mind tried to digest the idea; certainly from the faces he pulled he was chewing them round, spitting them out, then chewing them again.

'It's an idea worth thinking about,' he said. 'Might not go down well straight away but . . . '

Broke said goodbye to Crosland Page, Lizbeth, Gil Tander and the cowhands from the Lazy Z ranch. He'd said all he needed to his Pa and Tyler. He didn't return to the town of Hell. He rode out across the prairies.

THE END

We do hope that you have enjoyed reading this large print book.

Did you know that all of our titles are available for purchase?

We publish a wide range of high quality large print books including:
Romances, Mysteries, Classics
General Fiction
Non Fiction and Westerns

Special interest titles available in large print are:
The Little Oxford Dictionary
Music Book, Song Book
Hymn Book, Service Book

Also available from us courtesy of Oxford University Press:
Young Readers' Dictionary
(large print edition)
Young Readers' Thesaurus
(large print edition)

For further information or a free brochure, please contact us at:
Ulverscroft Large Print Books Ltd.,
The Green, Bradgate Road, Anstey,
Leicester, LE7 7FU, England.
Tel: (00 44) 0116 236 4325
Fax: (00 44) 0116 234 0205